Emerson's Adirondack Secret

Emerson's Adirondack Secret

by

Jeff Bigelow

Book design by Kiera Hufford
Cover design by Eric Frisino

Printed in the United States of America

The Troy Book Makers • Troy, New York • thetroybookmakers.com

To order additional copies of this title, contact your favorite local bookstore or visit www.shoptbmbooks.com

ISBN: 978-1-61468-498-5

ACKNOWLEDGEMENTS

Thank you to all my friends and family who have been with me through the good times and the bad.

A special thanks to Theresa Devane, Roger Bigelow, Christine Bigelow, Jillian Cooley, and Ashley Richardson. Your edits and suggestions were invaluable.

I would also like to thank *Peace Village* in Haines Falls, NY, as my inspiration for *Serenity Village*

Visit www.emersons-adirondack-secret.com.

Chapter 1

"Whatever you do, you need courage. Whatever course you decide upon, there is always someone to tell you that you are wrong. There are always difficulties arising that tempt you to believe your critics are right. To map out a course of action and follow it to an end requires some of the same courage that a soldier needs. Peace has its victories, but it takes brave men and women to win them."

~ Ralph Waldo Emerson

Saratoga Springs, NY – September 2028

"You need to get here right away. Your mother's in the hospital and it's serious."

"What happened?" Jasper asked.

"She took a blow to the chest during our protest," Jasper's father said.

"How did that happen?" Jasper got up from his seat at the kitchen counter and began pacing across the kitchen floor. He could read his wife's lips asking who he was talking to, but Jasper ignored her.

Jasper's father started sobbing. It was loud at first and then sounded farther away. Jasper guessed he was holding the phone away from his mouth. He had never heard or seen his father cry before and he was sure his father did not want him to hear him cry right now. Finally, his father said,

"Please just get here as fast as you can. We're at the George Washington University Hospital."

"OK, dad," Jasper replied. "I'll be there soon."

Jasper packed a few things for the hospital, gave his wife Sally a hug goodbye, gave Dakota a belly rub, and hopped in the car. Jasper's parents were lifelong Democrats but were never very active politically until they retired. During their retirement they started joining peaceful protests across the country whenever a group of individuals, usually the poor, were being abused or taken advantage of.

To try to control his racing mind, Jasper played the podcast he had been listening to earlier. It was fitting as it was about the events leading to President Ivanka Trump's recent decision to postpone the latest presidential elections that his parents were protesting in Washington, DC. Behind in the polls, Ivanka Trump had announced a state of martial law and the postponement of the upcoming presidential election due to a recent terrorist bombing at the Golden Gate Bridge in San Francisco.

Two terms were not enough for Donald Trump, so he had persistently pushed Congress to repeal the Twenty-Second Amendment that limits an elected president to two terms in office. Congress balked, but Ivanka Trump announced her candidacy soon after. Backed by her father and his supporters, Ivanka captured the Republican nomination and then squeaked into the presidency by barely winning the Electoral College but losing the popular vote by over 5 million votes.

~ ~ ~

About twenty minutes into the podcast, Jasper couldn't take anymore and turned it off. He needed to quiet his mind, so he turned on the New Age satellite radio channel and concentrated on his breathing as he tried to meditate. The meditation calmed Jasper and he was able to survive the trip as best he could.

At 2:00 a.m. Jasper walked into the intensive care unit waiting center at the George Washington University Hospital, where he saw his father sitting on a chair with his head in his hands.

"Dad!" Jasper said as he ran over to his father.

Jasper's father slowly lifted his head and looked at him. Tears streamed down his face as he reached over to hug Jasper. "Those bastards beat her for no reason."

"What happened?" Jasper asked as he sat down next to his dad. He had never seen his father like this. His dad was always in control, always stoic. But this had broken him.

"They came out of nowhere," Jasper's father said, fighting the tears back. "They drove right into the crowd with their trucks and didn't stop until too many people had piled up in front of them. Then they jumped out of the trucks and started swinging baseball bats and lead pipes through the crowd. They didn't care if they hit men, women, or even children."

Jasper's father broke down as he placed his head into his hands.

After a few minutes, Jasper's father raised his head. "I was able to shield your mother from one of the trucks as it came through the crowd, but the truck hit me in the back and I went down to the ground."

"Are you alright?" Jasper asked.

Jasper's father waved his hand in annoyance. "I'm fine. But as I was stunned on the ground, I saw one of the men climb out of the truck and head toward your mother. I tried to get up, but I had too many people on top of me…I tried to warn her, but it was too loud, and she was facing the other way…"

"Mr. Stone?"

Both Jasper and his father looked up to see a young female doctor standing next to them.

"Is this your son?" the doctor asked Jasper's dad.

Jasper's father nodded.

The young doctor motioned for Jasper to follow her and they both walked out of the waiting area to an empty hallway.

"I'm Dr. Devane," she said as she shook Jasper's hand. "I'm very sorry, but your mother experienced an extremely hard blow to the chest. The blow caused a pulmonary contusion and laceration, which is a bruising and tearing of the lung tissue. We attempted surgery to try to stitch the laceration, but the tearing and the bruising were too severe. She's stable now, but with her advanced age this has severely weakened her respiratory system. I'm afraid she could have respiratory failure at any time."

"Nothing can be done? Another surgery?"

"Nothing more can be done right now. We will just have to wait and see. I'm sorry," Dr. Devane said.

Jasper leaned over with his head in his hands and started sobbing. "It's not fucking fair," Jasper blurted out, finally accepting what the doctor was telling him.

After a moment, he raised his head up and tried to compose himself. "I'm sorry. Can I see her?" he asked.

"Please, don't apologize," Dr. Devane said. "I can take you to her."

Jasper followed Dr. Devane down the hallway. At the end of the hall, she opened a door for Jasper and let him in. As he walked in, Jasper saw his mother in the hospital bed. She had an intravenous drug drip inserted into her right arm and an oxygen tube inserted in her nostrils.

"She's in and out of consciousness," Dr. Devane said. "I will give you some privacy. Please come get me or call a nurse if you need anything."

"Thank you," Jasper said meekly.

As Dr. Devane left the room, Jasper sat down next to his mother and took her bandaged left hand. Jasper's mother had been his moral center all his life. Anytime Jasper got too proud or too selfish, she reeled him back in and reminded him to be humble and kind. She taught Jasper empathy, tolerance, compassion, and to respect all people, even people that he thought were evil.

Jasper wished he was as strong and brave as his mother, but he knew he was not. He was just as upset as his parents about what was happening to his country, but he had not done anything about it. He wanted to be as active and passionate as his parents, but something held him back. He was not sure if it was fear or apathy, but something was missing from him.

"Mom, can you hear me?"

Her head slowly turned toward Jasper and her eyes opened. "Jasper," she said weakly.

Jasper started to cry but forced himself to keep talking to her as he did not know how much more time he would have.

"Mom, I am so sorry I couldn't get here sooner. I am so sorry I was not a better son."

"It's alright Jasper," Jasper's mother said as she patted the top of his hand. "You're a wonderful son and a wonderful person."

Her grip loosened on Jasper's hands and her eyes started closing.

"Mom, please stay with me! Please..."

"It's OK." She squeezed Jasper's hand again. "It's just hard to keep my eyes open. How's your father?"

"He seems fine," Jasper said. "But he's worried about you."

"I know I'm dying. I can feel it. You must take care of your father. He's a good, strong man but has difficulty asking for help when he really needs it."

"I'll take care of dad," Jasper said. "But the doctors say you're OK and stable for now. We will fight this together and you will make it."

"Of course, we will," she said, but Jasper could tell she was only trying to make him feel better.

"And when you get better, we'll find the man who did this and make sure he faces justice," Jasper said.

"I'm not looking for justice," Jasper's mother said. "I'm only looking for peace."

"Can you tell me anything about the attack? What do you remember about the man who did this to you?" Jasper asked, trying to keep his mother awake and occupied.

"He had a mask on…I could not see much of his face… just a scar on his forehead…"

Her whole body went limp as the life in her fell silent.

CHAPTER 2

"To be yourself in a world that is constantly trying to make you something else is the greatest accomplishment."

~ Ralph Waldo Emerson

NEWCOMB, NY – OCTOBER 2035

As Jasper placed food and water bowls on the kitchen floor for Dakota, he felt his phone vibrate in his pocket. Palming his phone, Jasper's eyes widened at the text. Jesus, when was the last time he'd heard from Riley?

"I need your help. Contact me on my private Photive line as soon as you get this."

Riley Collins had been at school with Jasper in the geology department at Utah State and the archeology PhD program at Cornell University. However, just before their thesis defenses, Riley's father suddenly passed away and Riley left the program. Riley's father was a computer genius and a struggling entrepreneur who battled depression. After his latest idea was stolen by the Trump Administration, Riley's father killed himself with a shotgun blast to his head in his garage workshop. Instead of returning to school, Riley picked up his father's work and started his own company called Jordan, named after his father. Riley was extremely smart, like his father, but was more business savvy and a little more aggressive. Using his father's technology, he built his small startup into one of the most successful telecommunications companies in the world. His company specialized in secure long-distance communications, with his most commercial success being "Photive." Photive allowed secure, fast, and cheap video communications between anyone in the world.

Jasper got on his computer and called Riley on his private Photive line.

"Jasper, I need you to come to my house in Saratoga Springs as soon as possible," Riley said. His image appeared on Jasper's computer. Riley was dressed in an old, ratty, red Cornell sweatshirt that looked two sizes too big for him. Riley always looked like he just got out of bed. Half of his black mane was matted down while the other half stuck straight up at attention. Jasper mused that one of the many perks of being rich was that you could look and dress however you wanted, and no one would really judge you for it. They would call you "eccentric," but if you were poor, they would simply call you "weird."

"Nice to see you, too," Jasper said, smiling sarcastically. "But what is this about? We haven't talked in what seems like forever. Is everything alright?"

"Everything is fine," Riley replied as he took a drink from his Battlestar Gallactica mug. "I know we haven't talked in a while. That's partially on me, but you know you're not the best at keeping in touch either."

Jasper snickered. "I can't argue with that, but you know I'm always here for you."

"I know," Riley replied. "You know the same goes for me."

Riley and Jasper had been best friends in school and although they didn't speak often, they were always close. Jasper had helped Riley through the sudden death of his father, and Riley helped Jasper through the murder of his mother and the soon to follow death of his father. Although they didn't talk often, they knew they had each other's back whenever one of them needed it.

"I know," Jasper replied. "Before this becomes a mushy love fest, why don't you tell me what is going on?"

"I have a project I need your help with."

Riley left the running of his company to his employees, so he had time to pursue his passion for archeology. With no need for funding and no need to publish, he was free to study "fringe" archeological phenomena. His main passion was research on archeological inconsistencies that did not coincide with accepted archeological theories. Specifically, he was interested in finding alien artifacts that were believed to have been left by aliens visiting our planet in the past. Although there had been some interesting discoveries, like the Dropa Stones in Tibet and the Horned Human Skulls in Pennsylvania, they had all been debunked by respected archeologists. This was usually due to a suspicious lack of evidence. But Riley pushed ahead with his research. He had shared some of his theories with Jasper but was usually tight-lipped about any hard evidence he found. He was quite the conspiracy theorist as well and was always claiming he was being followed and tracked by some government or secret organization.

"Ah," Jasper said. "You need help with your latest wild goose chase."

"C'mon now. We are not going to have this argument again."

"Nope, we'll have it later," Jasper replied. "But if you need my help, I'll be there. But this better be at least interesting."

"How does a possible alien artifact in the Adirondacks sound to you?" Riley asked.

"OK, you got me interested," Jasper replied.

"Then I'll see you tomorrow?"

"Is it OK if I bring Dakota?"

"Of course. How is that little stinker doing?"

"Getting older but still pretty healthy," Jasper replied. "OK, see you tomorrow."

"Take it easy," Riley said, right before his image disappeared from the laptop screen and was replaced by the Windows 2030 logo.

Jasper had forgotten about his work responsibilities while he was talking to Riley. He had a federal job with the Northeast Republic that provided decent benefits but terrible pay, so to make some extra cash, he also worked part-time as a contractor. Although the Northeast Republic did not have much money, local Native American tribes still made money with their casinos and were willing to pay money to archeologists to find and dig up old artifacts. It was tedious work, but they paid well and were always excited when something was found. This was especially true if it showed evidence of their tribe in an area previously unknown to them.

Jasper scrolled through his emails on the tablet in the kitchen. No new jobs from the Native American tribes and no updates from the Northeast Republic. The Northeast Republic had put Jasper on temporary leave as they worked through their latest budget crisis. Jasper was hoping he would be able to work on some Native American digs during this time, but nothing was currently available.

After the Great Secession of 2030, the economy in the other five republics had suffered depressions. In comparison, the Northeast Republic was doing relatively well. The financial center of New York City contributed to the tax base and the Northeast Republic had been less ravaged by climate change than the rest of the former United States of America. But good jobs were hard to find, especially in strictly academic areas like archeology.

As Jasper put down the tablet and sat on the couch, Dakota jumped on his lap and started licking his face. Dakota was a Golden Retriever mix that Jasper had kept after his divorce two years ago. Jasper did not have to fight his ex-wife too hard for him. She was too wrapped up in her work and too focused on her social media standing to care about the dog very much.

Jasper took Dakota's leash, which made Dakota go crazy, put it on Dakota, and walked out the door. It was a chilly October evening as Dakota and Jasper made their way out of the small cul-de-sac and into "downtown Newcomb."

Because of its high elevation and northern location, the town of Newcomb remained even more intact than the rest of the Northeast during the change in climate that was happening. It was a beautiful mountain retreat that had to endure only its annual July-August infestation of city folk from New York City and Boston. Tourists from these areas were always a pain, but the tourist summer season was relatively short and was now over. Even though the winters were not as cold as they used to be, they were still too cold for most people. Plus, the mosquitos and ticks during the spring, summer, and now parts of fall also thinned the tourist herds.

As Jasper walked Dakota down backcountry roads for their typical scenic stroll downtown, his mind wandered as it often did on these hikes. Jasper was content with his quiet life and knew he was luckier than most these days. He was lucky to have a nice little homestead just outside of town. It was close enough to the cellular tower to get high quality phone and internet, but far enough away to have some privacy and peace and quiet. He had a small energy efficient house that needed only a little juice from Northeast Republic Power to supplement what he got from his solar panels and wind turbine. But something was still missing. After years of looking for his mother's killer, he became frustrated and had given up. He felt guilty about abandoning the search but getting information out of the Southern Republic was getting more and more difficult. Jasper was pretty sure his mother's killer lived there based on his previous research, but that theocracy's records were difficult to obtain for its own citizens, much less a "Yankee" from the Northern Republic.

Figuring he might as well give his cousins a heads up that he was heading out of town, Jasper ended up taking Dakota to the coffee shop in the center of the village. Comfortably Numb, as it was called, was run by his cousins, who made an amazing chocolate milkshake with a shot of espresso.

"Good evening, Jasper," Ken said, as he cleaned some pots behind the counter. Ken's eyes were even redder than usual. With the slowing of business in the fall, Jasper thought he must be smoking more weed now than he did when the summer tourists were in town.

"Hey Ken, how's it going?" Jasper asked as he walked up to the counter.

"Other than supply problems, not too bad. You want your usual?"

"Yes, please," Jasper replied. "Is it alright if Dakota comes inside?" During tourist season, Ken and Monica did not allow pets in the store because of fights between dogs and even between owners, but they made exceptions for locals during the offseason.

"No problem, I will probably lock up soon. Pretty slow today. Did you hear they're putting the Ten Commandments up at the courthouse?"

"I heard," Jasper rubbed his eyes. "It seems like there's always a big controversy about placing the Ten Commandments in a public place like a criminal court or some other state-owned property. I have no problem with that. Most of the Ten Commandments make sense—don't kill, lie, or steal—although some of them seem to show a rather insecure god. 'Thou shall not have any gods before me.' 'Thou shall not take my name in vain.' I can be insecure, but I really don't care if anybody likes other people better than me or uses my name as a swear word."

The forcing of one's personal religion down other people's throats really irked Jasper. He had grown up Catholic but strayed from the religion as he went to college. He strongly supported the freedom of people to worship however they please, as long as they didn't coerce or harm others. But mixing government and religion was dangerous. The founding fathers of the former United States knew that and specifically outlawed it in the First Amendment of the Constitution.

"So, I am fine with having the Ten Commandments posted anywhere. I simply think you need to have other people's beliefs posted there as well. You also should have the Five Pillars of Islam, the Four Noble Truths of Buddhism, the Four Aims of Hinduism, and finally the Eleven Satanic Rules of the Earth.

"By the way," Jasper continued, getting really worked up. "The Satanic rules pretty much boil down to don't hurt or fuck anything unless they plan to hurt you or want to fuck you first.

But you also must include the nonbelievers, the atheist and agnostics. Atheists are easy. Their plaque would say, 'Everything you see up here is bullshit. You are just a monkey with a bigger brain. When you die you become dirt.' You've got to love atheists, they make cross-fitters and vegans seem humble and nonjudgmental."

"I knew this would get you riled up Jasper, but Jesus Christ you're on a roll," Ken said as he finished making the milkshake.

"Finally, the agnostics, God bless them," Jasper continued, unabated.

"Or maybe not…" Ken added.

Jasper burst out laughing. "Good one. The agnostics' plaque would also be simple. It would simply say, 'I don't know, just don't be a dick.'"

"Wow, that was an impressive rant." Ken handed the milkshake to Jasper. "Anything wrong?"

After the death of his parents, his divorce, and his brother's move to the Pacific Republic, Ken and his wife Monica had become Jasper's closest family and friends. However, Jasper knew that Ken and Monica had their own problems and he did not want to burden them with any of his.

"Nothing in particular," Jasper said as he took a sip of the milkshake. "I guess a call I recently had from my friend Riley affected me a bit. He asked me to head to Saratoga to help him with something."

"Why did that bother you?" Ken asked.

"It made me realize what a rut I've been in over the past couple years. My career isn't going anywhere, my love life is nonexistent, and I've hit a dead end in my search for answers about my mother's death."

"You're too hard on yourself," Ken said as he sat on the stool next to Jasper. "You've gone through a lot in the last few years. I wouldn't describe it as a rut, I would describe it as a recovery period."

"I just wish I was stronger than this." Jasper tried to hold back tears. "I know people have suffered way more than me and have gotten on with their lives. But here I sit wallowing in my own self-pity."

"Don't compare yourself to other people." Ken placed his hand on Jasper's shoulder. "You're a sensitive person who cares about other people, animals, and the world in general. That's a good thing. But being sensitive also makes you more vulnerable to pain and uncertainty. It takes more time and more effort for someone as sensitive as you to recover from the terrible loss and betrayal you've had."

"Thank you," Jasper said as he wiped his eyes. "I don't know what I would do without you guys. I really appreciate the support you've given me."

"You're welcome," Ken said. "I know you find it tough to show any vulnerability, but we're always here when you need us."

"I know."

"Helping your friend with this new project might be exactly the thing you need," Ken said. "As John Holmes said, '*There is no exercise better for the heart than reaching down and lifting people up.*'"

CHAPTER 3

"It is one of the blessings of old friends that you can afford to be stupid with them."

~ Ralph Waldo Emerson

Jasper got up the next morning and loaded up his Trybrid SUV. Last night he had prepared the SUV for his trip by charging the battery, cleaning the solar panels, and filling the backup tank with gasoline at the local Stewarts. Hopefully, the sun would be out today, Jasper thought, so he would not have to burn any gas. The Northeast Republic had very high gas taxes as it was trying its best to wean people off all fossil fuels. At fifteen dollars a gallon, this strategy was working on Jasper.

Dakota loved riding in the car; he had been going nuts all morning watching Jasper pack the bags and load them into the SUV. Finally, after everything was packed, Jasper opened the back door and let Dakota in. A cage separated the trunk area of the SUV from the rest of the vehicle. Jasper knew if he let Dakota in the front of the car, he would be right in his lap, barking at the other cars and likely causing an accident. In the back, Dakota would be irritable for a while, but would quickly fall asleep to the gentle rumble of the drive.

Jasper pulled out of his driveway onto Route 28N for the hour and a half drive to Saratoga. As he headed south, Jasper noticed the color turning in the Adirondack trees.

The Adirondacks were affected by climate change (ticks, tree killing bugs, fires, etc.) but it was faring much better than the rest of the former United States.

At least the Northeast Republic was attempting to repair the environment and save a few public wildernesses. The Texas Republic and the Southern Republic did not even have an environmental department, or any public lands. Some wealthy private landowners in these republics owned large undeveloped areas, but this land served as sport hunting grounds for themselves or other wealthy citizens. These lands were poorly managed and were stocked with whatever remaining animals could be bought and transferred from other parts of the world.

Some people argued that it was worthless to try and save the last few remaining wild areas in the United States Republics or the world. They were all doomed due to climate change, many said. By the year 2050, it was estimated that all Earth's wild mammals over one hundred pounds would be extinct because of loss of habitat due to the expanding human population and climate change.

As Jasper hit Interstate 87 in Pottersville, he turned the car to self-driving mode. Although self-driving mode technically worked on the rural roads in the Adirondacks, Jasper did not trust it off the highways. The GPS and radar systems with self-driving cars had issues with the remote and forested area of Northern New York State. The forest sometimes blocked the GPS system and the radar system sometimes misread trees as buildings. This had caused many accidents in the Adirondack Mountains.

Traffic increased as Jasper arrived at Glens Falls and closed in on Saratoga. Traffic moved well as most people had their cars on self-driving mode, but there were always a few idiots that drove manually on freeways and mucked everything up. As they weaved back and forth across the lanes, they slowed down the conservative self-driving cars as they tried to avoid accidents and anticipate the manual drivers' next move.

Saratoga was the northernmost suburb of the growing Capital District. The moderate climate, abundant water resources, and relatively inexpensive real estate had drawn many transplants to the area in the last few years. Many city dwellers from New York City and Boston had grown tired of the constant coastal flooding and had moved farther inland.

Riley lived on a large piece of property just outside Saratoga. He built it as a compound where he could conduct business and host any business leaders or politicians he needed to see. His mother also stayed there sometimes, and she insisted that his property had horses she could ride when she got bored. Riley had zero interest in horses, but there were about ten people who lived on the property who bred, raised, and trained the thoroughbred horses he owned. Gambling endeavors, including horse racing and betting, meant big business in every United States Republic, and the famous summer Saratoga horseracing season was still going strong in the Northeast Republic.

After passing numerous surrounding farms, Jasper drove up to the front gate of Riley's property and pushed the buzzer.

"Hey Jasper," blurted the intercom.

"Riley?"

"Yeah, it's me. I will be happy to let you in but who would cross this bridge must answer me these questions three, 'ere the other side he see."

Quoting *Monty Python and the Holy Grail* was one of Riley's most annoying habits. Not that Jasper didn't like *Monty Python and the Holy Grail*—it was catnip for stoned college archeological students—but Riley drilled it into the ground sometimes.

"Ask me the questions bridge-keeper, I'm not afraid," Jasper replied.

"What is your name?"

"My name is Jasper Stone."

"What is your quest?"

"To seek the Holy Grail."

"What is your favorite color?"

"Blue. No yellow—auuuuuuuugh!"

Riley laughed as Jasper knew he would.

"Right. Off you go," Riley said after his laughter subsided. The gate opened.

Riley's property was gorgeous. Large green fields on rolling hills separated brown wooden fences with thoroughbred horses prancing and eating in the morning mist. Nicely spaced trees throughout the property accented the open fields and gave shade to the horses and the people tending them. As Jasper cleared the last rise on the road to the main house, matching brown buildings with solar paneled roofs glistened in the morning sun. The living quarters consisted of the large main house, two smaller guest houses, and two large garages. Further down the road were three large stables and two worker houses, all finished in the contemporary Adirondack wooden design.

As Jasper pulled up to the main house on the perfectly manicured circular driveway, Riley clumsily ambled out of house. Riley was tall, but skinny and completely uncoordinated. Although he never said anything about it to Jasper, it looked like one of his legs was longer than the other. He always seemed to limp when he walked. A stranger would never guess that he had money. Riley was very easy to talk to and never bragged or even talked about how much money he had. He did not own any expensive cars. This property was more for his mother than him. The only thing he spent money on was his passion for ancient alien archeology. Jasper admired him greatly, even though he thought his passion was a fool's errand.

"Glad you could make it," Riley said as Jasper stepped out of the car.

"Me too," Jasper reached for a quick bro-hug as the handshake merged into a hug.

"Come on inside," Riley said. "Sorry, but you'll have to put Dakota in the guest house. I don't care, but my mother doesn't want the dog in the main house."

"I understand," Jasper said.

"Why don't you put your stuff in the guest house, get Dakota settled, and meet me in the kitchen?"

"Sounds good. See you in a bit."

Jasper drove an additional five hundred yards to the guest house. From the outside, it simply looked like a smaller version of the main house. Jasper pulled up front, let Dakota out of the back, and took the luggage inside. Dakota was excited to be somewhere new and went about his smelling routine. Jasper gave him a beef bone from his treat bag to chew on and walked back to the main house.

Riley's main house was as beautiful inside as it was outside. It was large but not excessively so. It had five bedrooms and four baths. All the trim was done from Adirondack hardwood. The craftsmanship of the wooden trim and the dining room tables were noticeable even to Jasper's unrefined eye. An in-ground pool and a ground level recreation room with a pool table, entertainment center, and ping pong table rounded out the features of the house.

Jasper walked into the kitchen, where Riley was sitting at the kitchen table while his mother, Jennifer, was making sandwiches at the kitchen island. The kitchen was large and modern with granite countertops, stainless steel appliances, and a beautiful stone floor. Like the rest of the house, it was well built but not overly ornate or ostentatious.

"Jasper, it's so good to see you," Jennifer said. She gave Jasper a hug that lasted a bit too long. Jasper had a crush on Jennifer that he had always been very ashamed of. Jasper had a thing for older women, and Jennifer was one of the hottest older women he had ever met.

Jasper believed Jennifer was aware of his crush and purposely teased him whenever she could. She knew about Jasper's visit today and was wearing an outfit way too revealing for a sixty-year-old woman; her white tank top was about two sizes too small and barely able to support her very large, and very fake, breasts.

"Hello, Mrs. Collins. It's nice to see you, too," Jasper replied, trying to concentrate his gaze anywhere but her cleavage.

"Now, how many times have I told you to call me Jennifer?" She placed mini sandwiches and sodas on the kitchen table. "I'm so sorry to hear about your divorce. From what Riley told me, your ex-wife sounds like a real piece of work. But I'm sure a handsome man like you will have no problem finding someone new," she added with a quick wink.

"Mother," Riley said, staring at his mom like a nun would look at a misbehaving boy.

"Yes, yes, Riley. I'll leave you two alone now, so you can talk shop. I'll be out at the Canfield Stable if you boys need anything."

"Sorry about that," Riley said after Jennifer left the kitchen, closing the door behind her. "But I agree with her about Sally being a piece of work. You deserve someone better than that. How are you holding up? I know divorces can be difficult. I still haven't gotten over mine and that was five years ago. Yours was only two years ago."

"You know, it's not the divorce that was the problem," Jasper said. "For better or worse, I've always been somewhat of a loner and I have no problem being on my own. I also know I can be difficult to live with in that I need a lot of time alone, even when I'm in a close relationship with someone.

"It's the cheating and lying that gets to me," Jasper continued, the muscles in his face tightening. "I cannot believe the type of person she turned into."

"Did she apologize at least?" Riley asked.

"Not really," Jasper replied. "When she finally told me about the cheating, it wasn't until after we decided to get a divorce. And she said it in such a callous and cold way that I still am stunned by it. I wish I knew the truth right away, so I could have decided if I wanted to stay in the marriage or not. The worst thing is that I never got the chance to make that choice.

"I know people have lapses in judgement and make stupid mistakes. But either own that mistake and tell me about it immediately or take it to your fucking grave. Don't tell me about it in my weakest moment after you knew we were getting a divorce. I know relationships aren't fair, but they can at least be honest."

"Fuckin eh," Riley replied.

Riley and Jasper both laughed at the inside joke. Riley and Jasper played on the same hockey team at Utah State before they went to Cornell. They carpooled to and from games and practices together with two other friends, Magnus and Sudsy. It was a long way back from some of the games, so they decided to get a 6-pack of beer for the drive home. The next game it became a 12-pack and then it eventually became a 24-pack. They even had "jobs" for each occupant of the vehicle. The "Driver" did not have to drink and was allowed no more than two beers. The "Co-Pilot" had to help watch the road, scan for cops, and drink his fair share. "Beer Bitch" had to pass out the beers and drink his fair share. Finally, "Drunk Bitch" had to drink as much as possible.

The inside joke came from Riley when he was "Drunk Bitch" one night. When everyone was silent, he blurted out, "Fuckin eh." They all waited for some complaint or words of wisdom to follow, but that was all he said. When they asked Riley why he said, "Fuckin eh," he said he just felt like saying it. So, whenever Riley or Jasper didn't know what to say to each other, their default response was "Fuckin eh."

"I'm sorry." Jasper stopped laughing and took a mini sandwich off the plate. "I didn't come here for a pity party; you needed my help with your latest alien artifact. Is this one a crystal skull or some kind of large monolith?"

"Fuck you, smartass," Riley replied. "Before this argument starts, why don't we head out to the pool? It's a nice day and I think we both could use some sun."

It was a nice day and Jasper's butt had been getting sore sitting on the wooden chairs in the kitchen. Jasper followed Riley to the pool area after taking a few Labatt Blues out of the fridge. He had not been in a pool in a long time. Pools were quite the luxury now, and Jasper was hoping Riley would suggest a swim in the pool later. Twenty years ago, swimming in a pool in New York State in October would be cold and unpleasant. But now, warm falls seemed to be the norm.

Riley popped the cap off the bottle with a bottle opener nailed to one of pergola columns and continued the conversation as they sat down on some nice outside couches.

"I know you don't believe in my work, but I promise you I've researched some very interesting things. Unfortunately, I've come across some shady organizations that want to steal any proof I find."

"Who are these organizations and why do they care about alien artifacts?" Jasper asked.

"I think some of them are run by extremely wealthy assholes who want another trinket in their collection. Others could be governments or the United Nations afraid of public reaction to proof that aliens have visited this planet in the past."

"Why isn't there ever evidence of these finds?" Jasper asked.

"Well, I will admit that many of them are hoaxes," Riley conceded. "But the ones that are determined true quickly get stolen or hidden from the public. Either sold on the black market to the wealthy or hidden by government organizations."

"Well, isn't that convenient," Jasper said sarcastically.

"C'mon now," Riley replied. "I know you are open-minded enough to think that some of these artifacts have not been explained and are interesting. Like the Aiud object, the Human Horned Skulls, the Nazca Lines?"

"Yes, but all these potential alien artifacts have non-alien explanations," Jasper said.

"No, they all have non-alien theories," Riley replied. "Alien explanations were deemed too fringe, so archeologists had to come up with other explanations for these artifacts."

"What about the Oumuamua Object discovered in 2017?" Riley added. "Astronomers from Harvard University said it may have been an alien spacecraft. Their theory is based on the object's unexpected boost in speed as it traveled through and ultimately out of our solar system. They stated that Oumuamua could have been a light sail, floating in interstellar space as debris from advanced technological equipment."

"I remember that," Jasper replied. "But other scientists believed it was just a weird comet whose increase in speed was due to outgassing as it got closer to the sun."

Riley paused, rubbed his temples, and spoke slowly and carefully. "All I'm asking you to consider is this. Occam's Razor states that among competing hypotheses, the one with the fewest assumptions should be selected. For all these strange and 'out-of-place' artifacts that have been found all over the world, archeologists have had to come up with different assumptions to explain each of them. Weirder comets, more advanced metallurgy, higher creativity, and more complex technologies to move large stones—horizontally for Stonehenge and vertically for the Pyramids. What if you just made one assumption that ancient aliens with more sophisticated technology visited Earth in the past or have artifacts floating through space?"

"That's a pretty big fucking assumption."

"Is it really?" asked Riley. "Most respected space scientists believe there is life on other planets and a strong possibility of advanced civilizations with the potential for space travel. Isn't it possible that some of these civilizations could have visited Earth in the past? Maybe ancient humans thought they were gods? Perhaps an alien impregnated the Virgin Mary and that's why Jesus had such power and wisdom."

"Whoa, whoa, I am Catholic, remember. A Christmas Catholic, but still," Jasper retorted.

"I know, I know," said Riley. "Just yanking your chain. But there is some credible evidence in the Bible of some prophets describing potential alien astronauts."

"Bullshit!"

"Let me read you Ezekiel 1:4-6," Riley said, searching his phone. "Ah, here it is. 'I looked, and I saw a windstorm coming out of the north—an immense cloud with flashing lightning and surrounded by brilliant light. The center of the fire looked like glowing metal.'

"What does it sound like he was describing?" asked Riley, a shit-eating grin on his face.

"I have to admit, that does sound like a description of a UFO."

Riley continued reading. "'Also out of the midst thereof came the likeness of four living creatures. And this was their appearance; they had the likeness of a man. And every one had four faces, and every one had four wings. And their feet were straight feet; and the sole of their feet was like the sole of a calf's foot: and they sparkled like the color of burnished brass. And they had the hands of a man under their wings on their four sides; and they four had their faces and their wings. Their wings were joined one to another; they turned not when they went; they went every one straight forward. As for the likeness of their faces, they four had the face of a man, and the face of a lion, on the right side: and they four had the face of an ox on the left side; they four also had the face of an eagle.'"

"That could be describing aliens," Jasper said. "But that also sounds like he could be describing angels."

"So, is it easier for you to believe in angels than aliens?" Riley asked.

"Fair point. I guess I shouldn't be so quick to dismiss the possibility of ancient aliens," Jasper replied. "So, what have you found and why do you need my help?"

"Have you heard of the Philosophers' Camp?" Riley asked.

"Yes, from my dad," Jasper replied. "It was a meeting of philosophers in the Adirondacks during the 1850s, right?"

"Right," Riley replied. "In the summer of 1858, ten illustrious intellectuals went on a boating expedition to Follensby Pond near Saranac. The party consisted of Ralph Waldo Emerson, Louis Agassiz, James Russell Lowell, John Holmes, Horatio Woodman, Ebenezer Rockwell Hoar, Jeffries Wyman, Estes Howe, Amos Binney, and William Stillman. The rustic camp, which Stillman prepared, was situated between two huge maples, which inspired Lowell to name the site 'Camp Maple.' The guides, however, rechristened the place 'The Philosophers' Camp' and the latter caught on.

"William Stillman, one of the less famous people in the party, organized the trip and kept a journal of the discussions. He was most interested in Emerson and his belief in transcendentalism. Although Stillman published most of his notes, his actual journal was kept private and was left with his family when he died. An elderly colleague who was an expert in Adirondack folklore told me that he thought a strange object was brought to the Philosophers' Camp. The colleague died soon after he shared this information with me. So, I decided to buy Stillman's journal when his family put it up for sale."

"What did his journal say?" Jasper gasped sarcastically.

"The journal said that Emerson had found a strange object around Walden Pond and that he brought it to the Philosophers' Camp. Stillman wrote that Ralph Waldo Emerson told him it was the first time he showed this artifact to anyone. When he showed the artifact to the other campers, some thought the object was interesting and worth additional study. However, other members of the camp thought the object was only a rock and told Emerson to toss it into the water."

"Bullshit!"

"Do you want me to show you the journal?" Riley asked.

"You bet your ass I would," Jasper replied.

"OK, follow me."

Riley got up and headed inside. Jasper followed him until they reached a large metal door in the center of the house.

As Riley entered a code onto a keypad on the door, Jasper asked, "Where are we going?"

"You'll see."

After a faint click, Riley opened the door to reveal an elevator. Riley pressed his finger on the panel on the elevator door and it quickly opened. He walked into the elevator as Jasper stood outside the door, stunned.

"Do you want to see it or not?" Riley asked, turning to see Jasper standing still with his jaw wide open.

"What the fuck is this?" Jasper asked. He stepped one foot forward to look past the outside door to the elevator.

"I will explain, get in."

Jasper slowly walked through the door and into the elevator. The door closed behind him and Riley pressed the lowest button on the control panel. The elevator quickly jolted and moved downwards.

"I built this house over an old Atlas Missile Silo," Riley said turning to Jasper. "There were a lot of these built during the 1950s and early 1960s in Northern New York, but most were abandoned by the late 1960s. When this land went up for sale I jumped on it to have a safe place to store all my files and valuables. I had to refurbish it, but I tried to keep as much of the original stuff as I could."

The elevator stopped, and the door opened into a large room.

"How deep is this?" Jasper asked, stepping out of the elevator.

"It's about a hundred feet deep. This is the bottom level where I keep all my files and valuables. The upper levels contain living quarters and the old launch control room. I converted it all into separate apartments. I have about five apartments, each on different levels. Each one has a full bathroom and a small kitchenette. Ten people could live down here comfortably. It doubles as a fallout shelter if the world goes to shit. My family and I spent plenty of nights down here when it seemed like Donald Trump was going to start World War III with one of his late-night tweets."

As Jasper gaped at the large room, Riley put his face up to the wall on the other side of the room.

"What the hell are you doing?" Jasper asked.

"Just wait."

As Riley finished his sentence, the wall opened to a smaller room on the other side. Jasper had not seen the seam until the door opened.

"Face scanner," Riley said as he walked into the room. "The wall will only open if I put my face in the exact position."

"OK, that's pretty cool," Jasper said. He followed Riley into the room.

Riley walked to the back of the room and picked up an old journal off the shelf.

"No gloves?" Jasper asked.

"Using gloves for handling old documents is a myth perpetuated by movies," Riley said as he placed the journal onto the large table in the center of the room. "The problem with the white glove myth is that it fights against the very thing it is supposed to ensure—the safety of the historical treasure. Wearing white cloth removes any dexterity required when handling older paper. You are more likely to rip the document or bend it while wearing gloves of any sort. In addition, white gloves are more likely to sop up sweat and other oils that can then be transferred to the document. And the small fibers can be left behind and filed away with the document."

"Okay, sorry" Jasper said as he sat at the table.

Riley opened the journal. "Here, read this page."

Jasper leaned over and read the manuscript:

Mr. Emerson has brought a strange object with him from Walden Pond that he showed to the group this past evening. Mr. Emerson said he had found the object during one of his walks around the pond. It looked like a typical rock, except it was bright white and had one side that had a completely flat and reflective sheen. Although some of the group thought it was intriguing, Mr. Agassi, the only geologist in the group, told Mr. Emerson that it was only a rock dropped by the glacier during its retreat from Massachusetts thousands of years ago. Mr. Agassi thought Emerson should throw it into the pond as it would only be a burden on his trek home.

"Okay, that is interesting," Jasper admitted. "And he didn't include this in the published pieces of his journal?"

"Nope," Riley replied.

"So, you don't know if Emerson threw that object into the pond or kept it with him?" Jasper asked.

"Stillman was strangely silent on that point. The argument happened late that night and was the last part of his journal entry for that day. His journal continued the next morning and through the rest of the trip, but the artifact was never mentioned again."

"So, you think this artifact is at the bottom of Follensby Pond?"

"Possibly," Riley replied.

"So why do you need my help?" Jasper asked. "I assume you have the money and resources to hire a crew to scour that pond."

"I do, but I need more information. And I think your former girlfriend, Ingrid, has the information I need," Riley said.

Chapter 4

"Love, and you shall be loved."

~ Ralph Waldo Emerson

It had been fifteen years since Jasper had seen Ingrid, and five years since he had spoken with her.

"Ingrid! What does she have to do with this? She's in Chile!" Jasper said.

"Not anymore," Riley replied with a sly grin. He took a swig of his beer. "When the Northeast Republic was formed, they modified the immigration laws and allowed a certain number of 'spiritual advisors' to enter."

"Wow," Jasper said, shocked.

"Let me put this away and we can go back to the pool," Riley placed the journal back on the shelf. "It can get stuffy and a little claustrophobic down here."

As Riley closed the secret doors, Jasper's thoughts went to Ingrid.

Jasper had met Ingrid during graduate school at Cornell. Despite her name, Ingrid was not from Scandinavia. She was originally from Chile, where her family was poor, but her parents well-educated and worldly. Her parents taught her that despite their situation, she could be whatever she wanted. Ingrid took it to heart and decided at ten years old that she wanted to be a psychologist and live in America.

She was accepted to Yale with a full scholarship, and once in America Ingrid fell in love with two more things besides psychology: Ralph Waldo Emerson and the Adirondack Mountains. Every free weekend she had during her undergraduate work, she would load up her beat-up Subaru Outback with her kayak and a stack of Emerson essays and drive up to the Adirondack Mountains.

Once she finished her undergraduate work at Yale with high honors, she got another scholarship to Cornell for graduate school. Jasper met her in a creative writing class, an optional course for PhD students. Although they later could not decide who made the first move, they decided to meet up after he took Ingrid up on her offer to read his short story. When they met to talk about the story in the Cornell library, Ingrid admitted she had not read the short story yet and was very sorry. Jasper quickly forgave her, and they started talking like they had been close friends for years. There was no awkward small talk. They immediately jumped into talking about religion, travel, spirituality, personal faults, fears, and hopes and dreams. It took Jasper three dates to kiss her because he was afraid of ruining their friendship. But Jasper finally took a chance and he was glad he did.

Initially bonding over a mutual love of the Adirondacks, they grew even closer in the questioning of their Catholic upbringing and the constant search for spiritual truth. At Cornell, they took every hike worth taking and kayaked every stream worth exploring. During semester breaks, Ingrid followed Jasper back to the Adirondacks where they continued exploring the wilderness using Jasper's family's lake house as their base camp.

As Jasper followed Riley into the elevator, Jasper's thoughts became more depressing as he remembered how he lost Ingrid.

In their third year of graduate school, Ingrid's mother was diagnosed with breast cancer. Ingrid's father had died when she was in high school and she was an only child. There was no one else to take care of her mother, so she quit school and moved back to Chile to take care of her. Jasper visited Ingrid and her mother a few times over the next year, but the distance and time took a toll on their relationship. They kept in touch after their breakup and Ingrid's mother fought for two years before the cancer killed her.

Ingrid planned to come back to Cornell to finish her degree after her mother died but one huge obstacle stood in her way: Donald J. Trump. Donald Trump's unlikely election in 2016 led to a host of draconian immigration laws. One of those laws stopped international students from returning to school if they spent more than six months continuous time outside the United States. Ingrid had been gone for two years taking care of her mother. Both Ingrid and Jasper wrote dozens of letters and talked with numerous immigration officials before finally giving up. Jasper continued to write to Ingrid, but her correspondence became less and less frequent and more despondent.

The elevator returned to the top floor, and Jasper stepped out. "Ingrid is a spiritual advisor?" he asked.

"I guess so," Riley said as he closed and locked the elevator door. "She runs a Transcendental Meditation Center outside of Elizabethtown, New York."

Jasper was stunned. Why didn't she contact him? It had been a long time, but they had been so close.

"What does this have to do with your alien artifact?" Jasper asked.

"Well, I found out about her organization as I started to do some research on Ralph Waldo Emerson," Riley said, walking back toward the pool. "Their religion is partially based off Emerson's essays and lectures. Emerson was one of the first people to discuss transcendentalism principles. Therefore, this organization contains many of Emerson's published and unpublished works. When I called and asked them to transfer me to their resident Emerson archivist, who do you think answered the phone?"

"Ingrid," Jasper replied as they both returned to their original seats by the pool.

"That's right," Riley replied.

"Does she still hate you?" Jasper asked.

"She never hated me," Riley said. "She merely disagreed with every theory I ever had and was not afraid to tell me exactly why. Actually, it made me a much better scientist, although I would never admit that to her. She said she would show me her entire Emerson collection under one condition."

"What was that?" Jasper asked.

"That you and I attend her retreat this weekend."

"Ah, now I see."

"C'mon, it will be interesting at the very least. You're a spiritual seeker, right? In any case you get to see Ingrid."

One feature of the more progressive US Republics that had gotten stronger in recent years was a search for spiritual meaning. This search came in the form of new religions, new books, spiritual retreats, and even cults. Many people were having trouble dealing with the new world (and new countries) they were living in. Although the Great Secession of 2030 was mostly bloodless, it had decimated the economy and many people's families had been torn apart by the breakup of the United States.

Jasper stared off at the horse pasture as he thought about Ingrid and the retreat. In the pasture, there were three large horses standing in a circle all facing each other. They were not eating or nuzzling each other. They were simply staring straight ahead. It seemed like some invisible energy was drawing them together.

"Fine, I'll go," Jasper answered, looking away from the horses.

"Awesome, thank you," Riley said. "The retreat starts the day after tomorrow, so why don't you hang out here until then?"

Jasper agreed, and they toasted their agreement with a few more beers. They spent the rest of the day swimming, eating, and catching up. It was a nice day for both as they now had a purpose and a strategy to reach a goal. Riley's objective was the artifact. Jasper's objective was Ingrid.

Chapter 5

"When it is dark enough, you can see the stars."

~ Ralph Waldo Emerson

John looked through the binoculars, waiting for the last lights to turn off at the house. As he tried to concentrate on the house, his brother's lip smacking interrupted his train of thought. His brother, Mark, ate like a predator devouring his first meal in months. The only person he would work with now was Mark because he was the only person he could trust, but his brother's tics were sometimes more than he could handle.

"Could you eat that a little louder?" John mumbled.

"Fuck you," replied Mark. "You are the one who asked me to come on this job. I don't need the money. Why do you need me anyway? This place has almost no security with zero guards and only a handful of cameras that aren't even being monitored. Plus, you're only taking one unarmed civilian. You could do this job in your sleep."

"I brought you because of how much I love your company," John said sarcastically.

"Well, I know that," Mark replied. "But you also brought me because you're experienced, and you know that no job is as easy as it looks. You may be ugly, boring, and without any personality but you're safe and smart."

"Thanks," John said. "OK, last light was out about an hour ago. You ready?"

"Ready as I'll ever be."

John started up the van and drove it slowly along the fence line in electric mode to make sure it stayed quiet. He stopped as close as possible to the main house. John and Mark pulled on their masks.

"Remember, no casualties. And only use the stun gun if you absolutely have to."

"Yes, mother," Mark replied, stepping out of the van.

The fence was only six feet high and both John and Mark could climb over it easily. The fence was there to keep the horses from running away, not to keep out intruders. Mark and John kept low as they quickly jogged toward the main house.

Once they reached the side of the house they crouched down in the bushes. Using a simple flat ended screwdriver, John slowly started working the plastic strip around the windowpane in the bedroom window above him. John saw no lights in this bedroom, so he was pretty sure no one was sleeping inside. Even if someone was in the bedroom, John's years of experience kept this work quiet. After removing the strip, John started working on prying the windowpane loose from the frame. Finally, the windowpane broke free, and John carefully leaned the pane against the side of the house.

Yesterday, John had come to the house offering a free pest protection evaluation. After laying on the charm with one the girls working in the stable, she allowed him to circumvent the house where he said he would look for places that animals could get inside. Instead, John was able to confirm that the house contained no alarm system. It was a bit surprising, but he guessed the owner figured that the gate was enough protection in this relatively safe area outside Saratoga Springs.

John and Mark slowly climbed into the bedroom through the window. Taking their time, they both peered out the bedroom door to the hallway. Convinced that everyone in the house was still asleep, John lead Mark down the hallway into the bedroom of the target. The bedroom door was closed but revealed to be unlocked with a slight push by John. John pushed a little more and was relieved to discover that the door was relatively new with no creaking as he opened it fully. Clutching the syringe of Midazolam, John slowly approached the sleeping target with Mark following close behind. Without hesitation, John simultaneously put his hand over the mouth of the target while quickly giving him an injection in the shoulder.

The target spasmed for a second but did not open his eyes or mouth and quickly fell back on the bed. John removed his hand and checked the pulse. Perfect, he was alive but heavily sedated. The target would not wake up for another eight hours or so.

"Take his computer," John whispered to Mark, pointing to the laptop in the corner. "And grab anything that looks like a flash drive or a hard drive."

As Mark quietly seized the laptop and searched around Riley's desk, John slowly put the target over his shoulder in a fireman's carry position. Retracing their steps, John followed Mark out into the hall and back to the bedroom window they came in. Mark climbed out first and waited as John handed him the limp body through the window. Mark threw the body over his shoulder and John stepped through the window.

With Mark holding the target, John carefully replaced the strip and the window pane. Any detective worth his salt would easily be able to tell that there had been a break-in through this window even with John's careful work. But making the signs of a break-in less obvious would give them a few hours or even days of confusion before the police were brought in to investigate. Once John finished, they both started walking back toward the fence.

They continued across the horse pasture until they reached the fence. John climbed over first. Mark then heaved the body over his head, so the torso was on John's side and the legs were on Mark's side of the fence. John waited for Mark to clear the stone wall and then they slowly pulled the body back down to the other side of the wall.

Once the body was safely placed in the back of the van Mark asked, "Where are we taking him?"

"The client said to bring him to Lynchburg, Virginia where he'll meet us. So that's what we're going to do."

CHAPTER 6

"Life is a journey, not a destination."

~ Ralph Waldo Emerson

Jasper slowly opened his eyes as the morning sun broke through the shades of the cabin. He got up and headed to the bathroom. As he took a leak, he stared at himself in the mirror. Jasper had to admit he did not look bad for forty-five years old. His brown hair was thinning a bit, but most of it was still there. Jasper liked exercising and being active outdoors, so he was in solid shape. He could lose a few pounds, but his broad shoulders and large arms drew attention away from any minor amount of belly fat.

After brushing his teeth and taking a quick shower, Jasper started thinking about Riley's alien artifact. The little bit Riley had told Jasper yesterday had piqued his interest. Most of Riley's previous pursuits were overseas where "artifacts" had been found by uneducated rural villagers. When scientists would get to the site, the artifacts would either be obvious hoaxes, or lost or stolen. But the possibility that there was an alien artifact hidden in the Adirondacks, originally found by an individual like Ralph Waldo Emerson, was very interesting.

Jasper put on some clothes and took Dakota around the property for his walk. It was a bit chilly, and as he shoved his hands into his coat pockets, Jasper felt something inside the left pocket of the coat. He pulled out a small flash drive. It didn't look familiar, and he was pretty sure it was not his. Wondering where it came from, he put it back in his pocket and finished his walk with Dakota.

Once Jasper got back to the guest house, he took the flash drive out of his pocket and placed it on the desk in the corner of the house. Maybe it was an old flash drive he had forgotten about. The coat was old, and it could have been a flash drive he had put in there a long time ago. Jasper made a note to himself to check what was on it later.

After he fed Dakota, Jasper walked over to the main house and knocked on the door. Jennifer immediately opened the door, and she looked worried.

"Riley isn't here," Jennifer said. "His computer is gone, and all the cars are still here."

"Calm down, Jennifer," Jasper said. "He could've gone for a walk, or maybe someone picked him up and took him to a coffee shop this morning."

"No, no, no," Jennifer replied. "I looked at the video from the camera at the front gate from last night and this morning and no one entered or left the whole time."

"Is there any sign of a break-in?" Jasper asked.

Suddenly, Jasper remembered the flash drive he had found in his pocket. He told Jennifer he would be right back and ran back over to the guest house. Once inside, Jasper plugged the flash drive into his laptop and opened it. Inside were a bunch of files, including a large video file labeled "Play Me First."

Jasper clicked on the video and saw Riley's face.

"Hi, Jasper. I made this video the morning before you arrived at the house. I slipped this flash drive in your pocket as a security measure. I'd noticed a van parked outside the property for a few days and I was worried that someone was spying on me. So, I decided to put the most important files I had on the artifact on this flash drive and give it to you in case something happened to me. I know you think I'm paranoid, but better safe than sorry."

"I don't think you're paranoid anymore," Jasper said to himself.

"So, if something has happened to me, I do hope you'll continue my work and keep looking for the artifact. Let my mother and the police handle anything that may happen to me in the next few days. If you continue the search, you're more than likely to find me anyway. I know I'm asking a lot of you, but I really believe this find may change the world. Contacting Ingrid at Serenity Village is the next step. Please continue my work, I'm counting on you. Take care my friend."

Jasper closed the laptop and stared out the window. Two of the horses looked over the fence toward the guest house. Their intent stares made them appear to be waiting for the answer to the question Jasper was contemplating. What was he going to do?

Although Jasper had been dismissive of Riley's earlier pursuits, this one seemed different. There was Riley's disappearance, obviously, but Riley never would have asked him for help unless he really thought he had something. Riley had never asked him for anything. Jasper knew he needed to do this.

Jasper got up and walked back to the main house. Jennifer was now in the kitchen on her phone. Once she saw him, she told the person on the other line she would call right back.

"That was my sister," Jennifer said. "I told her that Riley was gone, and I didn't know where he was. She said she would come over. She only lives an hour away in Williamstown, Massachusetts."

"That's good," Jasper replied. "Riley left me a video message on a flash drive he slipped into my coat pocket yesterday. Do you know about his current project?"

"He has been vague about the details for some reason, but I know it has pretty much consumed him over the last few months. What did the video message say?"

"I don't want to worry you, but it seems Riley knew a kidnapping was a possibility. He said he wanted me to continue his research if he was taken and that may be the best way to find him."

"Are you going to do it?" Jennifer asked.

"Riley has never asked anything of me. I feel I need to do this for him. But I don't want to leave you and I don't want to stop searching for him."

"It's OK. Riley is a smart son-of-a-bitch and if he says continuing his work is the best way to find him, he's probably right," Jennifer said. "In any case, my sister is good in a crisis and she'll tell me the next step when she gets here."

"I hate to ask this, but could you take care of Dakota while I'm gone? I don't think it'll be safe for him if he comes with me."

"Of course," Jennifer replied. "I will watch him like he's my own."

"Thank you," Jasper said as he hugged Jennifer.

Jasper walked back to the guest house. Dakota was resting on the bed and wagged his tail as Jasper walked in the room. He sat next to Dakota and stroked his soft brown fur.

"I'm sorry boy, but I'm going to have to leave you here for a few days or maybe longer. I need to help a friend and I'm not sure it'll be safe for you with me. Jennifer and the staff here will take good care of you. I hope you understand."

Jasper knew Dakota didn't understand the words he spoke, but he did think Dakota could understand his emotions and how he felt. Jasper laid his head by Dakota and quietly cried into the bed. He was not sure why he was crying, but it felt like a release after what had happened over the last two days. He was worried about Riley and unsure that he could do what Riley had asked him to do. His usual anxiety and depression had been stifled by the action of the last 48 hours, but the minute he had time to think, it all came crashing on top of him.

Jasper had dealt with mild depression and anxiety most of his life. He got the depression from his father and the anxiety from his mother. What a great fucking combination. But these past years after the death of his parents and his divorce had been the worst of his entire life. It felt like a wet blanket had been placed on top of him and he could not get it off. Everything that made him happy before felt like nothing to him now. And little annoyances that he used to think nothing about now felt like the worst injustices in the world.

As he started thinking about Riley, Jasper was able to pull himself out of his malaise. Riley needed him and that was all that mattered right now. Jasper got up and opened his laptop. In Riley's flash drive file, Jasper found the number for Ingrid. Jasper pulled out his cell phone and dialed up the number.

"Om Shanti, this is Serenity Village. How may I help you?"

"Hi, I'm looking for Ingrid Black."

"One minute, please."

Jasper's mind, calmed for a few moments by his concentration on Riley and his mission, started racing again. He had not talked to Ingrid in five years. What should he say? Would she be mad at him?

After about a minute, a voice on the phone said, "This is Ingrid."

"Hi Ingrid, this is Jasper Stone."

"Jasper, it's so good to hear from you. Riley told me he would try to get a hold of you. How are you?"

"I'm good, but I need to tell you that Riley went missing this morning. He slipped me a flash drive before he disappeared, and I think he may have been kidnapped."

"Oh my God!" Ingrid replied. "I'm so sorry. What can I do? What are you going to do?"

"On his flash drive was a video asking me to continue his research on the artifact he was talking to you about. He thought that would be the best way for me to help him. I talked to his mother and she agreed with him. She said she and her sister would work with the police to find him."

"I think that's a good plan," Ingrid said. "Why don't you come here tomorrow morning, so we can talk, and I can show you what I have. I'm looking forward to seeing you again."

"I'm looking forward to seeing you, too," Jasper replied.

Chapter 7

"For every minute you are angry you lose sixty seconds of happiness."

~ Ralph Waldo Emerson

Lynchburg, VA – October 2035

After John handcuffed Riley securely to the chair, he pulled the bag off Riley's head and placed it on the table. Riley's eyes squinted as he tried to get used to the light. They were in a small office. Riley was handcuffed to a chair in the middle of the office and John sat at the back of the room. In the front of the room was a large oak desk with a middle-aged man sitting behind it. He was tan with thinning blond hair, and an obvious beer belly pushed out the bottom of his heavily starched white button-down shirt. A silver metal briefcase sat on the desk in front of him.

"Hello Riley," the blond man said as he pushed the briefcase to the side of the desk. "I hope the trip was not too hard for yawl."

Riley struggled to concentrate as he was exhausted. But he was not going to let this piece of shit make him acknowledge his weakness.

"Well, I've never been driven fourteen hours in the back of a locked van, given no food, and only let out once to pee and shit. So, I really have nothing to compare it to."

"I'm sorry about that," the blond man said. "Time is of the essence, and John here has little professional experience with communications or the service industry."

"Who are you?" Riley asked. "And what do you want with me?"

"Who I am is not important. What is important is what information you can give me."

"You're a Southerner," Riley said.

"How can you tell?"

"By your outrageous accent," Riley said. "What does the Southern Republic want with me?"

"Why do you think I'm with the Southern Republic? I could just be a southerner visiting the Northern Republic or originally from the south without losing my accent."

"Because all you Southern Republic officials look and sound the same. Like a cross between a lecherous preacher and a used car salesman. You're all sweet and nice to everyone in public, but secretly stab people in the back to keep your privilege and status."

"Ah, the charm of a Yankee," the blond man said. "Fine. I work with the Southern Republic. No reason to hide that. We're interested in the current artifact you're looking for. We scanned your computer and could find nothing of use. Why don't you tell me everything you know?"

"I'm not telling you shit," Riley said. "Why are you so interested in this artifact anyway? Investigating historical artifacts is about science and the search for truth. You guys run a theocracy where you teach that 'truth' can only be found in the Bible. Or that 'truth' is whatever Fox News South decides to broadcast."

John squirmed in his chair in the back of the room. He was from the Midwest Republic and did not like doing contract jobs for the Southern Republic. Like most people who lived outside the south, he thought the Southern Republic was a racist theocracy run by "good old boy" white southerners who had never stopped fighting the Civil War. The independent news reports of voter suppression, police brutality, and the mistreatment of minorities in the Southern Republic were very disturbing. But this was a well-paying job when there weren't many of them out there anymore. His number one concern was taking care of his family. Everything else was secondary.

"Let's just say we think your artifact may have some religious implications," the blond man replied. "If we knew what it meant, we would be able to guide our citizens on how to interpret its spiritual meaning."

"You mean lie to them," Riley replied. "Doesn't matter. I hit a dead end anyway. It was only another hoax based on some old stories."

"Among the many assets of being a good liar is being able to easily tell when someone else is lying, especially someone who is inexperienced in deception," the blond man said. "But I'm not worried; we will get the truth out of you."

"So, are you going to torture me? I knew what I've heard about the way you run things down south were true. Don't bother, it'll be a waste of your time. Like I said, it was just another hoax."

"Please, Riley. We're not going to torture you. We've learned after much experience that torture doesn't work, especially in these types of situations. You'll end up sending us on a wild goose chase for an artifact that does not exist and waste our time," the blond man said. "But thanks to our Russian allies, we have a chemical that will make you voluntarily tell us what you know and what you were planning on doing next."

Riley had no witty retort this time. The new Russia Alliance was known to have very effective techniques to get the truth out of its prisoners. Riley was scared and was having difficulty hiding it now. He would fight the effects of the serum as best he could, but he knew it probably would be a lost cause.

The blond man opened the suitcase and pulled out a large syringe filled with a clear liquid.

"This might sting a bit during the injection, but you will feel amazing afterwards," the blond man said as he walked over to Riley. "You'll experience a sense of total trust in humanity as your fears melt away, and I will seem like your best friend to whom you can tell anything."

As the needle penetrated his neck, Riley hoped that Jasper would follow through on the leads and information on the flash drive he slipped into his jacket the other night. Riley also hoped that Jasper would stay safe.

CHAPTER 8

"What lies behind us and what lies before us are tiny matters compared to what lies within us."

~ Ralph Waldo Emerson

SARATOGA SPRINGS, NY – OCTOBER 2035

Jasper spent the rest of the day talking to Jennifer and her sister about what to do about Riley's disappearance. They notified the police once Jennifer's sister, Michelle, arrived at the house. The local Saratoga County police said they could not open an official missing person's report for 48 hours, but they would come by tomorrow and unofficially start their investigation.

In the evening, Jasper started going through the files on the flash drive. There wasn't much to go on. There had always been a certain mystique about the Philosophers' Camp in the Adirondacks due to the amazing group of people who attended. Despite the name that became associated with the meeting, the men were not necessarily philosophers by training or occupation. The party consisted of two poets, Ralph Waldo Emerson and James Russell Lowell; two scientists, Louis Agassiz and Jeffries Wyman; two lawyers, Ebenezer Hoar and Horatio Woodman; two doctors, Estes Howe and Amos Binney; John Holmes, the younger brother of writer Oliver Wendell Holmes, and William James Stillman.

William James Stillman, an artist, writer, and skilled woodsman who had made many trips to the Adirondacks, organized the meeting. Stillman also had the most authoritative account of the meeting, which he published in the *Autobiography of a Journalist.* There was nothing of interest in Stillman's accounts of the meeting. It mostly highlighted the study of local flora and fauna, an appreciation everyone had for the beauty of the place, and some highlights of philosophical discussions around the campfire.

However, Riley had found Stillman's original journal which had some additional information that was not included in his published book. Stillman was a big admirer of Emerson and spent the most time with him at the camp. Stillman was a lost soul who was having trouble finding meaning or direction for his life. During the retreat, Stillman was constantly around Emerson trying to probe his deepest thoughts. The two men shared a common interest in nature, philosophy, and hypothetical subjects such as extra sensory perception and transcendentalism.

Riley had also written notes on how Emerson had left clues about the spiritual and supernatural experiences he had during Philosophers' Camp in his poem *The Adirondacs*. This poem was published soon after his trip to the Camp and was dedicated to his "fellow travelers."

The poem was very long and described normal activities conducted at the Camp like hunting, listening to the loons, and the general enjoyment of nature and his companions. But Riley was more interested in the more esoteric parts of the poem.

Riley had underlined the following part of the epic poem:

The other slow, —this the Prometheus,
And that the Jove, —yet, howsoever hid,
It was from Jove the other stole his fire,
And, without Jove, the good had never been

Riley noted that in some traditions Prometheus made the first man from clay, while in others, the gods made all creatures on Earth, and Prometheus was given the task of endowing them with gifts so that they might survive and prosper. Feeling sorry for man's weak and naked state, Prometheus raided the workshop of Hephaistos and Athena on Mt. Olympus and stole fire, and by hiding it in a hollow fennel-stalk, he gave this valuable gift to man which would help him in life's struggle. Prometheus also taught man how to use this gift and so the skill of metalwork began; Prometheus later came to be associated with science and culture.

Riley wildly extrapolated this part of the poem and its mention of Prometheus to be a hidden message from Emerson on the object he had found at Walden Pond. Riley thought that Emerson was trying to say that the object he found was from the heavens and was gifted to him to help him understand the truth of life and how to share this truth with others. As Emerson was one of the leading writers of his day, Riley thought that Emerson believed the object was specifically "placed" near Walden Pond so Emerson could share its secrets with the world in his own respected prose.

"Wow," Jasper said out loud. Riley had one hell of an imagination. Jasper admitted to himself that Stillman's unpublished journal entry about the object was interesting, but Riley's interpretation of Emerson's poem about his time at the camp was a huge stretch.

Jasper read Riley's notes and files until he couldn't keep his eyes open any longer. At 10:00 p.m., he turned out the light, petted Dakota, and dropped off to sleep. He dreamt of huge Greek Gods coming after him with lightning bolts.

CHAPTER 9

"Fear always springs from ignorance."

~ Ralph Waldo Emerson

ATLANTA, GA – OCTOBER 2035

"Yoga is a system of spiritual control practiced in both Hinduism and Buddhism. By means of the discipline's techniques of breathing and other exercises-control of the senses, meditation, and withdrawal-the person involved is led to a blissful union of self with the divine.

"In other words, yoga is a direct 'slam' against the Christian faith. If one can, by using special yoga breathing techniques, connect oneself to God, then why did Jesus die on the cross? Yoga claims to do what only Jesus Christ can do! The Bible says our sins have alienated us from our Lord. Your sins have torn apart the original relationship God lovingly intended to exist between Him and you.

"Centuries and centuries ago people were impressed by sorcerers and spellbinding preachers, etc. Today, this deception continues in cults like yoga. Why is this great deception of the devil so effective?

"Now people want something to ease their tensions in life, stimulate their physical wants, and give them a bit of heaven now and then. Therefore, there is little doubt that many people in the other republics are flocking in large droves to things like yoga -- a very anti-Christian cult or other new age blasphemy. These people do not want to be bothered by God's clear revelation in the Bible that they are sinners. Most of us don't want to repent. So, we flock to other things.

"If you are looking around for some spirituality more exciting than the historic Christian faith, be very careful. You may be one of the millions for whom yoga, mindfulness, or meditation is quite inviting. If this is the case, think very carefully about what you are doing. The stakes are high. See, if you are a follower of these cults, when you come to the end of your earthly existence, be prepared to call on them to rescue you from the curse of your sins.

"Do not believe these lies that come from outside this blessed Republic. They are told by heathens and unbelievers who are trying to remove God from your lives. Our evangelical Christian beliefs are the only true path and the only true religion. In Jesus Christ you have the forgiveness of all your sins, plus the absolute guarantee of being in Paradise with God forever! Amen."

Joel Robertson finished his sermon to thunderous applause from the thirty thousand people in attendance at the Trump Auditorium in Atlanta, Georgia. It was the culmination of a beautiful nondenominational Christian service on a sweltering October day. Yankees would have called it a political rally, but Joel thought of himself as a pastor first and a member of the Christian Conservative Party second.

As Joel sat down in the green room, he poured himself a tall glass of Jack Daniels and looked at the messages on his two phones. One of his phones was his official phone that he used for his capacities as a pastor, the Secretary of Religion for the Southern Republic, and his duties as husband and father. The other phone was used for "unofficial matters." This included correspondence with his girlfriends and communication with his undercover contractors.

Joel had learned his lesson about keeping separate phones right before the Great Secession. He was arrested by the FBI on charges of domestic terrorism after being implicated in the bombings of abortion clinics and assaults at counter-protests across the former US. They had confiscated his only phone, which contained texts and emails of his correspondence with local cells of the former Alt-right and Christian revenge movements. Luckily for Joel, one of the agreements of the Great Secession was the allowance of a certain amount of pardons for each new Republic. As an influential pastor in the south, he was granted a pardon at the request of the newly formed Southern Republic. After a few years of "repentance," he was given his current cabinet position.

As the "Theological Leader" of the Southern Republic cabinet, it was his job to keep the population of the republic happy and prevent them from fleeing to another republic. This mainly consisted of leaking reports to Fox News South that made the Southern Republic look good and the rest of the republics look bad.

It was easy to make the other republics look bad. All the US Republics were suffering from food shortages, destruction of ecosystems, and economic decline. However, trying to find anything positive about the Southern Republic was difficult. In addition to hardships shared with the other republics, the Southern Republic was constantly deluged with hurricanes and other major storms. Flooding on the coastal cities was commonplace. Miami, Savannah, and Charleston were in a constant loop of destruction and rebuilding after each hurricane season.

Without any natural resources other than the decreasingly less productive oil rigs in the Gulf of Mexico, the Southern Republic had to import most of their metals, coal, and natural gas. Way behind the other republics in renewable energy, the

Southern Republic was having issues keeping the lights on as the resources of natural gas and coal continued to dwindle.

The elimination of the minimum wage and the repeal of most gun laws had brought about a two-tiered society. The rich lived in beautiful neighborhoods with large houses and private police forces, while the poor struggled to survive working slave wages and avoiding mass shootings, which happened about once a week.

Every new Southern Republic president promised to solve the inequality through continued decrease in taxes and reduction of regulations. This, however, continued to make problems worse, as the rich could find loopholes to avoid most taxation while the poor struggled to pay their taxes and stay healthy in the toxic air now present in all the larger southern cities. Farming was the Southern Republic's largest industry, but even that was in decline due to the chaotic weather that challenged farmers with long stretches of alternating floods and droughts.

Finding scapegoats for these problems was getting harder and harder for Joel and the other leaders of the Southern Republic. The government was almost completely controlled by the Christian Conservative party. The party, in close partnership with the Christian megachurches, had a stranglehold on the presidency and controlled over 75% of Congress. The Southern Republican and Southern Democrat parties lagged far behind the Christian Conservative party. Immigrants were no longer an easy target, as the republic was losing more people than they were gaining. Although the terms of the Secession Treaty of 2030 had allowed free movement across the republics for two years after the treaty was signed, the borders of each republic closed quickly after that. Many minorities and non-Christians who had stayed in the Southern Republic during the first few years were now fleeing it in droves because they feared for their lives and their freedoms.

As Joel scanned the most recent economic data looking for some good news, his secretary opened the door to the green room.

"Mr. Robertson, Mr. Oscar is here to see you," Ashley said.

Ashley was a young blonde woman who had recently graduated from Oral Roberts College with a degree in political science. Under the direction of the president, cabinet members were "encouraged" to hire young, good-looking women as their secretaries. The official reason was that it would distract any official from other republics or countries before a meeting. But Joel understood President Donald Trump Jr., and knew there were other reasons.

"Send him in," Joel said.

Billy Oscar worked for Joel as a contractor. As the Theological Leader, Joel was also in charge of spying on the rest of the republics to protect the Southern Republic from any outside influences that could threaten their theocracy. Christianity was the official religion of the Southern Republic and only Christians could hold major political offices.

Joel oversaw the mission of obtaining information about any anti-Christian movements either inside or outside the republic. This included the discovery of any artifacts or any other scientific discovery that could threaten the Christian doctrine. Although the Southern Republic was unable to stop most scientific progress outside its borders, having information about it beforehand allowed them to discredit the discovery before it was made public. As for archeological artifacts, the Southern Republic had been successful in obtaining many artifacts they deemed dangerous to their dogma. Billy was tracking one of these artifacts now and was coming in to give an update on his progress.

"Good morning, Mr. Robertson," Billy said as he entered the room.

"Good morning," Joel said. "Please sit down."

"Thank you." Billy sat in the chair across from Joel's large desk. "I have some additional information on that artifact I've been tracking."

"This is the one that may be an alien artifact?" Joel asked.

"Yes. At first, I was skeptical, but I recently obtained some additional information that makes me believe that it could be real."

"Do you have any idea where it is?" Joel asked.

"Not yet," Billy said. "But we're currently following a few leads based on some recent intelligence."

"Why should we be concerned about this artifact... if it even exists?" Joel asked.

"For a couple reasons," Billy replied. "First, if the artifact is confirmed to be alien in origin, then it proves that there is other intelligent life in the universe. This would confuse our Christian citizens who would wonder why God would have made other intelligent life on other planets. Our special place in the universe would be threatened.

"Second, the artifact seems to have a close connection with Ralph Waldo Emerson. He either found it or was in possession of it at some time."

"Who is Ralph Waldo Emerson?" Joel asked.

"Emerson was an American essayist, lecturer, philosopher and poet who led the transcendentalist movement of the mid-19th century. He was initially a pastor, but gradually moved away from the religious and social beliefs of his church. Emerson discounted biblical miracles and proclaimed that, while Jesus was a great man, he was not God. He was staunchly opposed to slavery and believed that the Civil War was a righteous battle between good and evil."

"I take it he thought the Old Confederacy was evil," Joel said.

"Yeah," Billy said. "Strange thing is, for much of his early life, Emerson was silent on the topic of race and slavery. Not until he was in his late forties and fifties did he become known as an antislavery activist. This is right at the time that our information tells us he encountered the artifact."

"Are you trying to tell me that this supposed alien artifact pushed this Northern academic to be opposed to slavery?" Joel asked.

"Just a theory I have. Actually, it's a theory that one of the researchers said while he was being..."

"Stop," Joel interrupted. "I do not want to know anything about your information gathering techniques."

"Plausible deniability," Billy said. "I get it."

"OK, you've convinced me this is something we need to be concerned about," Joel said. "Continue following your leads, but do not interfere until you believe they've found the artifact or you believe they're no longer useful. The rest I will leave up to your discretion."

"Of course, thank you for your time," Billy said as he got up from his chair. He knew what Joel's last sentence meant. Get the artifact using any means necessary.

Chapter 10

"It is not the length of life, but the depth."

~ Ralph Waldo Emerson

Saratoga Springs, NY – October 2035

Jasper woke up early the next morning in a sweat after one of the weirdest nights of dreams of his life. Like always, he remembered only bits and pieces. One dream was about having trouble finding a classroom in college and being worried about being late. He had these types of dreams before, but this one seemed to have taken place in the 1800s and he was looking for Dr. Emerson's class. In another dream, he was being slowly chased by five creatures, each as tall as a typical NBA center, but dressed in black hijabs. Like all other chase dreams, when he tried to run, he felt like he was running in molasses.

Jasper took a shower, packed up his stuff, and walked Dakota over to the main house. He knocked on the door and Jennifer opened it up.

"Are you sure it's OK that Dakota stays in the main house?" Jasper asked.

"Of course," Jennifer replied. "It's not fair to leave him in the guest house. He'll be good company for me and my sister. I'll take care of him like he's my own."

"Thank you so much," Jasper said. "I'm heading up to Elizabethtown to follow a lead. I'm not sure when I'll be back."

“Okay,” Jennifer replied. “Please be careful and let me know what you find out.”

Jennifer gave Jasper a hug and took Dakota’s leash.

“Goodbye boy,” Jasper said as he kneeled and kissed Dakota on his head. “You be good for Jennifer and I’ll be back soon.”

Jasper loaded up his Trybrid and got back on I-87 to get to Elizabethtown. It was about an hour and a half drive. He turned on the news; he had not kept up with it over the last few days and was curious about what he had missed.

The news was as bad as it always seemed to be. Monster hurricanes continued to crash into the Atlantic Coast of the Southern Republic. Many cities along the coast like Miami, Savannah, and Charleston had been temporarily abandoned due to constant storm surges. But the Southern Republic would not give up trying to move people back into their constantly flooding coastal cities. They were bound and determined to prove to their citizens that climate change was not real by calling these monster hurricanes and floods “acts of God” and they continued to try to rebuild these cities even as they were underwater half the time. The Southern Republic government continued to deny climate change, even as their people were more affected by it than any other republic.

The Texas Republic, the Mountain Republic, and Mexico continued to have fights over water access in the region. Militia groups from each area, secretly funded by each government, were constantly sabotaging new wells and aqueducts of their neighbors. The North America Military Alliance would sometimes try to step in and keep the peace, but they were stretched too thin to make any real difference.

China continued its economic and military dominance. China announced that week that it had met its goal of being powered 75 percent by renewable energy resources by 2035 and was on track to be at 100 percent by 2050. Although

China was the leader in renewable energy, it continued massive coal, gas, and oil extractions in Asia and Africa. These resources were then sold to Russia, the US Republics, and South America. The Great Secession of 2030 severely weakened US presence in the region, so Japan, Australia, and other smaller countries were now under China's control. The Asian Alliance included token amounts of other countries' militaries but was run by China.

Jasper turned off the radio and decided to enjoy watching the countryside for a while. None of the leaves had turned yet and it was mid-October. When Jasper was growing up, he remembered the leaves in the Adirondacks would be past peak by now. One of the reasons he decided not to have kids was that he was not optimistic about the future, especially since he appreciated nature and animals so much. Large land mammals all over the world were disappearing at staggering rates. Birds could keep up with the changing climate because they were mobile. Trees and plants were somewhat successful because their seeds could be transported by birds to more northern or higher elevation locations. Most plants were being affected by invasive species, especially by insects like bark beetles and ash borers that were destroying huge amounts of forestland. In addition, forest fires were now prevalent throughout the US. Up until about ten years ago, there were only forest fires in the west, but now eastern forests were catching on fire in the hot summers due to the droughts and dead trees killed by climate change and its related invasive insect infestations.

Jasper was lost in thought and almost missed the turn off I-87 at the Elizabethtown/Westport exit. The meditation center was about ten miles off the freeway outside of Elizabethtown. When Jasper arrived at the center, he parked the car in the visitor parking lot and walked up to the reception area.

Their main building was beautiful and looked like a fancy golf clubhouse from the outside. It was a one story, long building with a plain white façade. It had a large wooden deck surrounded by many beautiful flowers. Jasper was not sure if the flowers were fake, but they smelled good and at least looked real at first glance. A few middle-aged men and women were sitting on the deck enjoying the morning sunshine.

Inside, the building was even more beautiful, with a sparkling white reception and information desk. Jasper walked up to the reception desk where an older Indian woman with beautiful long white hair sat, looking over a computer.

"Hello," Jasper said.

"Om Shanti," she replied.

"I'm here to see Ingrid Black," Jasper said.

"One minute please," she said as she reached for the phone. As she spoke in a foreign language, Jasper scanned a pamphlet about the retreat center.

WELCOME TO SERENITY VILLAGE

There are spaces that touch the heart and soul in ways that you will not find anywhere else. Serenity Village is a learning and retreat center that offers weekend retreats on a variety of topics where you can learn to meditate and study spiritual knowledge. The silence and tranquility of the Village provides the atmosphere for self-exploration and spiritual practice. Practicing yogis and spiritual advisors volunteer and teach at Serenity Village. Their hospitality and joy while hosting you during your retreat will be one of the memorable aspects of your stay. We opened in 2020 and are a retreat center of the Brahma Kumaris and the Emerson Transcendentalists.

Join us for weekend residential retreats, workshops, and weekly classes in spiritual awareness, meditation, and the practical application of spirituality.

As Jasper read the pamphlet, he started pondering his own spiritual beliefs. Although he grew up Catholic, he had given up on the church due to its social policies. He was not an atheist but was open to any ideas or beliefs that he could be talked into. Recently, most of the smartest scientists and thinkers in the world were convinced that we were all part of a computer simulation. Or even a computer simulation within a computer simulation. It was a miracle that during the breakup of the US there were no major battles or launches of nuclear weapons. After the Great Secession, rumors swirled about near misses that were avoided only by the strangest of circumstances.

Therefore, the current theory among scientists was that the entire universe is a simulation and "God" is the manager or managers of the simulation. They proposed that humans are like cells (or bacteria) within a human body. The body cannot live without the cells, but the body does not care about individual cells within the body. There are trillions of cells and bacteria within a human body. However, when enough of the cells become diseased, like with cancer, then humans become concerned and try to do something about it.

"God" does the same thing. When there are too many bad people, God orchestrates a purge of the bad people that are hurting the larger universe body. However, these purges are blunt and destroy good people just like chemotherapy destroys good cells in addition to cancerous cells.

This new belief system was called Virtualism. Virtualists believed that one could see this truth through deep meditation. Some even claimed to have achieved this state, but they were short on details and their claims were quickly debunked.

Jasper looked up from the pamphlet to see Ingrid walking toward him. Ingrid had aged very nicely and was still the beautiful woman he remembered. She was medium height with long black hair and deep brown eyes. Even under her very modest robe, you could tell she was a classic Latino, with curves in all the right places.

"Hi Jasper, it's so good to see you!" she said as she gave him a hug. She smelled like a mix between wild flowers and shampoo, a fresh, clean scent that was very pleasant.

"It's so good to see you, too," Jasper replied as they separated. It was a hug just long enough for old friends, but not long enough for former lovers. Jasper was a bit disappointed.

"I'm so sorry about Riley," Ingrid said. "Have you heard any news or have any idea where he could be?"

"Unfortunately, no," Jasper replied. "Riley's mother is working with the police and said she would call me if she gets any information. I'm following Riley's wishes and moving ahead with his quest, so to speak."

"I know it's tough, but I think you're doing the right thing. You have no idea what happened to him and you'll be doing no good sitting around worrying about him. Continuing his quest is what he wanted, and you should do it. Plus, it may turn out to be a way you can find him."

"Thank you," Jasper said. "Your opinion still means a lot to me, and it really helps to have your support."

"No problem," Ingrid replied. "I wish I could do more. I was about to eat breakfast. Are you hungry?"

"I could eat," Jasper replied.

"Why don't we get breakfast in the cafeteria?" Ingrid said. "But I have to warn you that it's all vegetarian."

Jasper laughed. "I guess I'll have to suffer through it."

As they walked to the cafeteria, Ingrid shared some information about the village. The retreat was run by about fifteen people, all women. Their retreat center was originally part of a larger spiritual movement based in India called the Brahma Kumaris. The Brahma Kumaris was a worldwide spiritual movement dedicated to personal transformation and world renewal. It was founded in India in 1937 and was committed to helping individuals transform their perspective of the world from material to spiritual. It supported the cultivation of a deep collective consciousness of peace and of the individual dignity of each soul.

However, about five years earlier, the Brahma Kumaris started having financial troubles and Serenity Village was threatened with closure due to a lack of money. Ingrid had kept in touch with the head of Serenity Village, Ella Wanzung, after they met at an international mindfulness conference in India. When Serenity Village was being threatened with closure, Ella contacted Ingrid. Ingrid had just been given a green card from the Northeastern Republic for her work with the Emerson Transcendental Society. Ella invited Ingrid to join Serenity Village where they could do retreats together for both of their organizations. Ingrid accepted, and with the money brought in by the Emerson Transcendental Society, Serenity Village was now in the black.

The Transcendentalist movement had a lot in common with the Brahma Kumaris. Both empowered women and were pillars of social justice. The transcendentalists led by Emerson pushed for women's suffrage and the abolition of slavery, and the Brahma Kumaris were started by a man in India who chose women to run the organization, and people from any caste were invited to join.

Both had core beliefs in the inherent goodness of people and nature. They also both believed that society and its institutions had corrupted the purity of the individual, and both belief systems had faith that people could become their best selves when they could calm their minds, live in the moment, and free themselves from their selfish animal instincts. In addition, Emerson was one of the first American intellectuals to research Eastern belief systems, especially Buddhism.

As they walked to the cafeteria, Ingrid also gave Jasper a tour of the main building of the campus.

"To your right is our main large auditorium and classroom," Ingrid said.

The auditorium was a large carpeted room with high ceilings and a medium-sized stage at the front. There were five rows of chairs arranged in a semi-circle surrounding the stage and six tables placed along each side of the room with about seven chairs per table. It looked like a typical banquet or wedding hall apart from the two portrait paintings on the left side of the stage and one huge photograph on the right side of the stage. On the left was the founder, an older man of Indian decent with a slight smile and a well-trimmed mustache. The picture below the man was a frumpy older Indian woman with jet black hair tied back in a tight bun. On the right was a good looking, clean shaven, older gentleman with perfectly coifed black hair parted to the side.

"Who are the people in the portraits?" Jasper asked.

"On the left are Brahma and Mama," Ingrid replied. "They are the founders of the Brahma Kumaris. C'mon Jasper, you know who the guy on the right is."

"Oh right," Jasper said. "That must be Emerson."

"Ralph Waldo Emerson," Ingrid replied in a very proud tone. "One of the greatest thinkers of all time. Not bad to look at either," she added with a wide smile.

"And I thought your interest in him was spiritual all this time," Jasper said. "Now I realize you only had the hots for him."

"Just a bonus," Ingrid replied as she continued the tour.

They continued walking through the main building to a small lobby with a few couches and tables.

“This is the reading room and over there is the small classroom,” said Ingrid as she pointed to the adjacent room. “Our smaller retreats use this classroom while our larger retreats use the large auditorium.”

They reached the cafeteria. The cafeteria was relatively plain with approximately thirty tables, a coffee and tea bar on one side of the room, and a short food service buffet on the other side. The remaining walls were windows with an amazing view of the Adirondack Mountains. Jasper followed Ingrid to the food service area, which could have been taken directly out of Jasper’s high school. Two older women in white robes handed each of them a small bowl of plain oatmeal with raisins and exactly four orange slices. Jasper picked up some utensils, a napkin, and some coffee and sat down next to Ingrid. Ingrid explained that the morning classes were starting in about a half hour, so the cafeteria was quite busy as the students and teachers got something to eat beforehand.

“We try to get as much of our food locally as we can,” Ingrid said as she very slowly started eating her oatmeal. “But sometimes the costs or availability of the food requires us to get some of our food from larger food suppliers. However, all the food we serve is certified organic and vegetarian. We believe a vegetarian diet aids in creating a tranquil state of mind. We also believe that the avoidance of alcohol, tobacco, and non-prescription drugs helps keep the mind light, alert, and able to understand aspects of spirituality more deeply.”

Jasper nodded as he dug into the oatmeal, which was admittedly quite good. The coffee was a bit weak but tasty. As he let his eyes wander around the cafeteria, Jasper noticed a huge map on the wall showing the locations of all the Brahma Kumari and Transcendental centers around the world.

“Wow, I had no idea your organization was that big with so many locations,” Jasper said as he pointed to the map.

"Yes," Ingrid replied. "We have more than one million regular students, with over 8,500 centers in one hundred countries. The only place we are lacking centers is in the Middle East and the Southern Republic. The religious zealotry in both those areas make it too dangerous for us to try to form centers there."

This seemed to be the jumping off point for Ingrid as she started to tell Jasper about the Brahma Kumaris and their history.

The founder, Fathera Lekhraj Khubchand Kripilani ("Brahma Baba") was a wealthy jeweler who was respected in the community for his piety. He reported having a series of visions and other transcendental experiences that commenced around 1935 and became the basis for the discourses. He believed there was a greater power working through him and that many of those who attended these gatherings were themselves having spiritual experiences. The majority of those who came were women and children from the Bhaibund caste—a caste of wealthy merchants and business people—whose husbands and fathers were often overseas on business.

The organization gave very special importance to the role of women and did not adhere to the caste system. It named a twenty-two-year-old woman, Radhe Pokardas Rajwani ("Mama"), as its president, and her management committee was made up of eight other women. People from any caste could attend the meetings. The group also advocated that young women had the right to elect not to marry, and that married women had the right to choose a celibate life. In tradition-bound patriarchal India, these personal life decisions were the exclusive rights of men.

During Ingrid's history lesson, relaxing music started playing from the sound system within the cafeteria. The minute the music started, Ingrid stopped talking and closed her eyes. As Jasper looked around, he noticed everyone else had stopped what they were doing as well. Everyone stopped eating, the food servers stopped serving food, and anybody walking in or out of the cafeteria stopped dead in their tracks. Some people stared straight ahead, while others kept their eyes closed. The music went on for about a minute and then slowly faded out. Once it faded out, everyone picked up where they left off and continued on their way.

"Sorry, I forgot to tell you about that," Ingrid finally said. "We call that traffic control."

"What's traffic control?" Jasper asked.

"It's our way of taking a minute each hour to be mindful and meditate," Ingrid replied. "Our minds can start racing around when we're busy. The traffic control stops and calms your mind, so you can relax and actually concentrate on the present moment and not dwell on the past or worry about the future."

"I could use that," Jasper said. "My anxiety takes hold of me too easily these days with all that's changed."

"Well, perhaps I can help you with that," Ingrid replied. "I know you're eager to look at Emerson's archives, but I must be with you while you look at his research."

"Okay," Jasper said.

"It's not that I don't trust you, I trust you with my life. But it's the village rules that no one can be in the archival library without someone else present."

"That makes sense."

"I need to run a part of a retreat today. Since you can't look at the archive until tonight, I was thinking you could attend some retreat classes? It could help you with your anxiety and maybe even help you on your spiritual journey."

"That sounds like a plan," Jasper said. He was always open to hearing new spiritual perspectives, but he thought this place, although beautiful, gave off a bit of a cultish vibe.

"Don't sound too excited about it," Ingrid said. Jasper never lied to her, or to anyone else for that matter, but she could always tell when he was holding something back.

"Sorry, I'm a bit nervous about this place, but that's not fair. I've only been here for fifteen minutes and it's not fair to judge something so quickly. I would love to sit in on your retreat."

"OK, thank you," Ingrid said. "I think you'll like this place after today. A class starts in the big classroom in about fifteen minutes. Classes will continue for the retreat all day. I recommend you attend all of them. I need to get some things together before the retreat starts, so I'll meet you at the end of the day."

Fifteen minutes later, after taking a peaceful walk around the grounds, Jasper entered the large classroom. The room seated about a hundred people in seven rows and about half the seats were filled. As Jasper took a seat in the back row, an older woman turned on the monitor and sat down in front of the room without saying a word. The large screen on the back of the stage lit up and a picture of a white point of light radiating light all around it on a bright red background was projected on the screen. Very relaxing new age music started playing over the speakers in the auditorium. The music had no words, but pleasant light interludes of flutes and guitars over a slow keyboard background.

The screen slowly scrolled through beautiful nature scenes: a flowing mountain stream in the morning light, a sunset over a mountain lake, a snow-covered mountain. It was very peaceful, and Jasper enjoyed this peaceful moment of reflection. Inspirational quotes also flashed on the screen every few minutes. It was very calming and relaxing, and Jasper was slightly perturbed when the screen went blank and the music stopped.

The older woman who had turned on the music and screen picked up a microphone from a table nearby and welcomed the audience to the retreat, called "Meditations for Inner Peace and Greater Power." She introduced herself as Mary Jean and said she had been with the Brahma Kumaris for seven years.

As she talked about her life, Jasper looked around at the other people attending the retreat. It was a broad and diverse mix of people. White, African-American, Indian, Asian, old, and young. Probably twice as many women as men. All seemed attentive and very concentrated on what Mary Jean was saying.

After Mary Jean finished her preamble and everyone introduced themselves, Mary Jean introduced topic of the early morning class of the practice of meditation. Mary Jean and the other instructors stressed how important it was to meditate every day, not just when you feel stressed. They said the constant practice of meditation will help train your mind and help you deal with outside influences in your life.

After a brief break, the late morning presentation was about how consciousness works. They taught that the consciousness was made up of three different parts: mind, intellect, and personality. Everyone has a King, or Raja, that is meant to control all these different parts. They stressed the importance of paying attention to what our consciousness is doing and making sure that the Raja is keeping a balance over the three parts of our consciousness. If our Raja is allowed to slack off, one part of consciousness will take over and dominate thoughts. Usually, it is the mind that takes over and leads to constant worry about future events and rumination over past events. Practicing meditation can train you to be in control of your thoughts, strengthen your Raja, and allow you to attain inner peace, clarity, self-control, and realization.

They also used the idea of a garden as a metaphor for your spiritual being. In starting a garden, you first need to pull out the weeds. For your spiritual garden, you need to first remove all evil, greedy, and selfish thoughts from your mind. Once the weeds have been removed in a garden, you must plant good things like fertilizer and seeds to start the healthy growth process. For your spiritual garden, you also need to add good things like gratitude, knowledge, love, and peace. Finally, you need to tend a garden by making sure it has sun and water to help it grow, and you need to pull any weeds that may resurface. With your spiritual garden, you need to control your thoughts and meditate to keep it healthy. You also must be aware of bad thoughts that may creep into your mind and remove them. Just like you would remove weeds from an actual garden. If you let the bad thoughts grow, they will choke out the good plants and seeds that you need for a healthy spirit.

After a quick vegetarian lunch, everyone returned to the same classroom for additional lectures. The afternoon lectures concentrated on using meditation and cultivation of a positive internal soul to connect to God. The instructors said that thoughts can go to two different places: 1) To the Outer World of people, jobs, relationships, and senses; and 2) To the Inner World of God, memories of your soul, and feelings of the heart.

They taught that this connection to God can provide stability in a world of constant change. Their concept of God was very new age-like and nonspecific. They described God as an ocean of pure water you want and need a connection with. They described God as an energy of pure love and peace who resides in a realm of light that is the home of all souls. This world is only a stage where humans are actors who play their parts wearing the costume of the body. Meditation purifies the inner soul allowing it to connect to the subtle non-physical dimension where they experience God's presence and the truth about the soul's journey.

CHAPTER 11

"Adopt the pace of nature: her secret is patience."

~ Ralph Waldo Emerson

Jasper met Ingrid outside the library after a decent dinner of vegetarian chili in the cafeteria.

"So, what did you think of the retreat?" Ingrid asked.

"I actually liked it a lot," Jasper said. "Some of the stuff was a bit New Age but a lot of what they said made sense and I think it actually will help me with my anxiety and depression."

"I thought you would appreciate it," Ingrid said smiling. "What about the spiritual side of it?"

"I liked that, too," Jasper said. "I think there's a real possibility you can see the truth through meditation and looking inward. It makes sense that we all have this spiritual connection to each other through a 'God' that is the source of all life and goodness. The only thing I had trouble with was their idea that all souls are inherently good, and that it's only the soul's attachment to social constructs and the outside world that corrupts us."

"Why don't you believe in that?" Ingrid asked.

"Well, as a scientist it seems to totally ignore the inherent animal instincts that humans are born with. Whether we like to admit it or not, we all have strong instinctual desires to survive, become strong and powerful, and to procreate. It's important that we try to control these instincts with our conscience and intellect, but these are natural tendencies we have as animals. So, I think a belief that we are inherently good may be a bit misplaced."

"Interesting," Ingrid replied. "Believe me, I would love to argue with you, but I'm sure you're eager to look at the Emerson Archives."

"Yes, but I'm also looking forward to the argument," Jasper said.

"Me too," Ingrid said, smiling. "The archives are in a building on the other side of the complex. However, this is our silent hour. So, we must walk over there in silence."

As they walked in silence toward the archives, Jasper thought about how he missed the deep conversations he and Ingrid had shared together. When they were a couple, they would regularly stay up almost all night discussing philosophy, religion, spirituality, and anything else that would flow through their heads. Although they agreed on a lot of topics, it was always more interesting to argue and try to persuade the other person. Both of them were open-minded and they each were sometimes successful in changing each other's minds.

~ ~ ~

Jasper specifically recalled one night in graduate school when Ingrid talked him out of atheism. Jasper had just finished reading all the older atheism books of the early 2000s like *The God Delusion* by Richard Dawkins and *God Is Not Great* by Christopher Hitchens and was convinced that there was no God and all religions were only a natural adaptation for enhancing the reproductive success of the species. Jasper confronted Ingrid with this point-of-view, his evidence drawn from his scientific background, these books, and common sense. She did not strike back with her own belief. Instead she asked him a series of questions.

The first was, “Has there been a published and reviewed scientific paper that proves there is not a God?” Of course, there wasn’t, so Jasper had to concede her point there. But he argued there also was not a published and reviewed scientific paper that proved there was a God. She agreed with that point and then asked, “Well, then shouldn’t you have an open mind about it until you see conclusive evidence for either theory?”

Jasper had to admit she had another good point, but he still wanted to be right, so he replied, “Well, although there is no conclusive evidence to prove there is not a God, many other scientific theories lead us to believe there is not a God, or at least no need for one to explain our existence. The Big Bang Theory explains how matter came to be formed and led to the formation of stars and then planets that could sustain life. The Theory of Evolution then explains how we evolved from simple one-celled organisms to plants and animals and eventually humans. So scientific evidence can explain our existence without a God,” Jasper argued proudly. “What evidence do you have that there is a God?”

Ingrid paused and thought for a second. Once again, instead of having a retort, she asked Jasper another question.

“OK, do you feel there is something more to you than biology?”

“What do you mean?” Jasper asked.

“Well, if there is no God, you’re only a biological creature. Granted, a smart biological creature with strong sociological and technical attributes, but a biological creature none the less guided by instinct, evolution, and environment.”

“That’s oversimplifying it a bit, but I guess I agree with that,” Jasper replied.

"What I am asking is, do you feel there's more to you than that? Do you feel the deep love you have for your parents is only an evolutionary response? I know you would die for them, even though that would be the wrong thing to do biologically. They're no longer able to procreate while you are. You dying for them does not help perpetuate the species."

"That's just one specific example," Jasper retorted.

"Do you believe the way your favorite song moves you is just a biological reaction? Do you believe that the feeling you get when you watch a sunset over an Adirondack lake, or watch a dog you shared twelve years of your life with pass away, or the love you feel for me are only evolutionary responses or biological reactions?"

"OK, I get your point," Jasper finally relented. "I do feel, once I get past the vanity of myself, that there is something more than biology and evolution inside myself and in others. But you're fighting pretty dirty adding my love for you in your argument."

"Anything to win the argument," Ingrid said with a smile. "Are you OK if we call this something, spirituality?"

"Yes, that's an acceptable, although not quite accurate, term," Jasper replied.

"So, is it that hard to believe that it's possible we're connected to each other through some central entity or power in these universal feelings of love, sacrifice, and spirituality?"

"No, it's not," Jasper had conceded.

~ ~ ~

As Ingrid unlocked and opened the door to the library, Jasper so wished they could have those talks again someday, but right now he had to concentrate on Riley and his mission.

The retreat's library was more like a bookstore with a private library in back. In front, they sold mostly self-help books on meditation and mindfulness. They also sold some New Age novels and historical books about religious and spiritual movements through history.

The Emerson archives were in a special collection behind the main library. The door to the special collection was locked, and Ingrid used another separate key on her keychain to open it.

The inside of the collections room was small and well-organized. Two large bookshelves covered two walls of the small room. These shelves were filled with old books, journals, and loose manuscripts. A small wooden table was placed in the center of the room with two chairs and a box of gloves. The other wall opposite the entrance door contained a large painting of about ten men at a rustic camping spot in the woods.

As Jasper walked over to look at the painting, Ingrid spoke up, "That painting is *The Philosophers' Camp in the Adirondacks* and was painted by William James Stillman. It used to be at the Concord Free Library in Massachusetts, but they lent it to us when the library flooded during Hurricane Kristin in 2027."

"Stillman was the one who organized the trip, right?" Jasper asked.

Ingrid nodded, "Yes, he was the organizer but they all used Adirondack guides to get them in and out of the deep woods."

As Jasper looked closer at the painting, he remembered Riley had an entire folder of files about this painting on the flash drive. Jasper had been thinking of Riley all day as he attended the classes at the retreat. Although he knew he was doing what Riley wanted him to do, Jasper was still worried about what happened to him and where he could be right now.

The Philosophers' Camp in the Adirondacks,
William James Stillman, 1858
Concord Free Public Library William Munroe
Special Collections

Jasper sat down on the table and pulled out his laptop. "Riley had some notes about this painting," he said as he opened the hard drive and then the folder labeled "Philo Camp Painting."

The folder contained multiple picture and text files. There also was a large video file labeled "Conclusions."

Jasper figured they might as well watch that first, so he clicked on the file.

A video screen popped up with Riley in the foreground and an easel in the background holding up the painting *The Philosophers' Camp in the Adirondacks*. Jasper pressed play.

"Hello, Jasper. Hopefully I'm with you when you're watching this video, but I thought there might be a chance that I wouldn't be. Who knows, perhaps Ingrid is there with you or us. Hi, Ingrid, if you're there."

Riley waved and both Ingrid and Jasper chuckled.

"I hope you're watching this video because you're looking at the original *The Philosophers' Camp in the Adirondacks* painting completed by Stillman. I know it's in Ingrid's Emerson Archives because I called the Concord Free Library and they told me they lent it to you. If you don't have the painting in front of you, please hit pause and get it online. It doesn't have to be the original, but it would great if it was."

Riley took a sip of water and picked up a pointer, and Ingrid and Jasper looked at each other puzzled but hopelessly amused. A few seconds later, Riley restarted his "lecture" by using his pointer to highlight different parts of the painting behind him.

"This painting is more than a record of the 1858 Philosophers' camp. It represents Stillman's interpretation of the significance of that outing. Although Emerson's figure does not dominate the painting, he is in the center of it due to Stillman's respect and awe of him. Behind Emerson on the left is a cluster of campers grouped around scientific naturalist Louis Agassiz, who is supposedly dissecting a fish. On the right of Emerson, a group of marksmen engage in target practice under Stillman's direction."

Riley continued, "I want you to pay attention to two parts of this painting. First, notice Emerson. Emerson stands alone in the middle, soaking up the wild majesty around him, in contrast with his busy fellow campers, who are preoccupied with the concrete reality of nature. Stillman's Emerson is moved by his immersion in the virgin forest and responds to it in a deeper, more spiritual way than the other campers. Emerson was always interested in the spiritual and he was especially introspective during this outing.

"Second, please look at the group of campers on the left. According to Stillman's journal, that's Agassiz dissecting a fish while four other campers watch him. But look closer. Is that what it looks like? What is that bright white rectangle? Why are four people watching him dissect a fish? All of them were sportsmen and had very likely seen the inside of a fish before. Although Agassiz was a biologist, he was also a geologist. Stillman mentioned in his private unpublished journal that Emerson brought a strange rock-like object to the camp. It would make sense that Agassiz would be the one to analyze it, since he was the only geologist on the trip. It also makes sense because Stillman mentions in his unpublished journal that about half the group thought the object was interesting, while the rest of the group thought it was just a rock."

A wry smile grew over Riley's face, and Jasper was sure he was about to make a wild assumption. Instead he made a request. "Please stop this video and look closer at the object Agassiz and the others are looking at. After you have taken a good look at it, restart the video."

Jasper hit pause and both Ingrid and Jasper got up and looked closer at the painting. It was strange something that white was brought on a camping trip. It looked perfectly square and was propped up on a stump. Jasper had no idea what that object could be in 1858, but if it existed in a current picture or painting he would have a pretty good idea what it was.

"So, what do you think it looks like?" Ingrid asked.

"I don't know," Jasper said. "Why don't you tell me what you think?"

"You know I can tell when you lie," Ingrid said, smiling broadly. "You do it so rarely and so poorly I think anyone could tell. Anyway, I asked first, so I think you owe me your opinion."

"Fine," Jasper said. "I know it's not possible, but it sure looks like a computer tablet."

Jasper expected Ingrid to burst out laughing, but instead she looked confused and anxious.

"Well shit," she said. "I was hoping you would come up with something that made visual and historical sense because I sure as hell was not able to. The whole time I was looking at the painting, I tried to come up with something possible, but all I kept seeing was a computer tablet or a laptop."

"Fuckin Riley," Jasper said. "That sonofabitch hooked us like two young and dumb stocked brook trout just dropped out of the plane."

"Yep," Ingrid agreed. "Let's see what he says."

Ingrid and Jasper sat back down in front of the laptop and Jasper pushed play. Another shit-eating grin crawled over Riley's face as he continued his lecture.

"So, what do you think? Sure looks like a computer tablet, doesn't it? I wanted to stop and make sure you had it in your head already, so you couldn't accuse me of putting it there. Probably still didn't stop you from calling me a sonofabitch though."

Riley continued, "Well, unfortunately, that's all I have now. I hope you can find the next clue in the Emerson archive. Good luck and may the force be with you." He smiled and put up his right hand with the Live Long and Prosper sign that Spock used on *Star Trek*.

"Isn't that hand signal from *Star Trek*?" Ingrid asked. "Why did he do that after saying a line from *Star Wars*?"

Jasper was strangely attracted to Ingrid in that moment she knew the difference between *Star Wars* and *Star Trek*.

"Because he's a sarcastic motherfucker," Jasper replied. "He knows the difference and is just fucking with me."

Chapter 12

"Do not go where the path may lead, go instead where there is no path and leave a trail."

~ Ralph Waldo Emerson

"Well, I guess I better get to work," Jasper said.

"You mean, WE better get to work," Ingrid replied.

"You want to be part of this wild goose chase?" Jasper asked.

"Now I do," Ingrid replied. "I admit when Riley first told me about what he was looking for, I thought he was just on another one of his crazy theories. But after he was likely kidnapped for what he knew, and after looking closer at that painting, I'm curious. Plus, with Emerson being in the middle of this crazy conspiracy, how I can walk away?"

"It will be great to have your help," Jasper said. "I guess we should start with any journals he has from the Philosophers' Camp trip. Do you have any of those?"

"I have it organized by year so that would be 1858," Ingrid said as she started to flip through the books and journals on the bookshelf.

"Have you read everything that's in here?" Jasper asked.

"Most of it," Ingrid replied. "I haven't gotten the chance to read through some of the newer material we received."

"Newer material?" Jasper asked. "You're still finding new writings and materials from Emerson?"

"Yes. Once people found out we moved his archives up to the Adirondacks, some of his extended family who live here have given us some of his personal letters or other unpublished works.

"Here are we are," Ingrid said, pulling out a stack of papers. "I actually have not read much of this. We received these pretty recently from one of his descendants."

Ingrid put the stack on the table, and Jasper grabbed half the stack and put it in front of him. Ingrid took the other half of the stack.

Hours went by as they painstakingly went through it all. Jasper was looking through some of Emerson's personal journals when he found the journal Emerson brought with him to the Philosophers' Camp. His journal about his time there was filled with great joy. Emerson was not much of a sportsman, but he enjoyed learning about the strategies of hunting and fishing. He especially enjoyed the comradery between all the intellectuals and guides.

Emerson especially enjoyed the solitude and peacefulness of the Adirondacks. The organizer of the expedition, Stillman, seemed to understand this and took Emerson on hikes and paddles to the quieter parts of Follensby Pond. Emerson's writings about the Philosophers' Camp were mostly descriptions of the people that accompanied him on the trip and the beauty of the camp. Although Emerson had known many of his fellow campers well before this trip, the wilderness had unlocked aspects of their characters he had never seen.

Jasper found that Emerson's journal of his trip to the Philosophers' Camp was a joy to read and exhibited what an amazing man Emerson was. Emerson was an extremely open-minded individual who was always willing to re-evaluate his beliefs based on new facts and information. Always curious, he asked many questions of others and himself to try to understand things more clearly. His perpetual wonderment and lack of vanity and self-importance was obvious in his writings.

Although reading Emerson's journal was interesting, Jasper was not finding any hints or information about the artifact that Riley had discussed in his research. Emerson's journal moved to documenting his trip home, and Jasper thought that he should move on to some of the other archives, but he decided to continue reading a little longer.

On his way home, Emerson stopped by John Brown's farm in North Elba. John Brown was an American abolitionist who believed and advocated that armed insurrection was the only way to overthrow the institution of slavery in the United States. Emerson was also a fervent abolitionist and became friends with John Brown after they met in Concord, Massachusetts in March 1857. In 1848, Brown heard of Gerrit Smith's Adirondack land grants to poor black men and decided to move his family among the new settlers to lead the freed slaves in farming the area.

John Brown was in Kansas at the time of the journal, but Emerson stopped by to see John's family and visit with the black families farming in the area. As Jasper continued to read about Emerson's discussions with the farming community, he said out loud, "Holy shit."

Ingrid looked up from the old newspapers she was scanning through, "What is it?" she asked.

"You've got to read this," Jasper replied. Ingrid pushed her chair next to Jasper's and leaned over the journal.

"Start right here," Jasper said, pointing halfway down the page:

After enjoying a wonderful dinner of pork and potatoes, five of the local farmers and myself sat in the kitchen and enjoyed smoking our pipes. The farmers were devout

Christians but started sharing their doubts with me about Christianity. While they were slaves, their owners had indoctrinated them in the southern plantation owner's version of Christianity. Every Sunday, they read them Bible verses and preached to them the importance of following the rule of God and the law. The plantation owners specifically chose Bible verses and sermons stressing that their toils in this world would be rewarded in the life to come after death. Any desires they may have had to better their current situation would not help them now or in the afterlife.

However, because of their new-found freedom, these black farmers had started to question their faith. They still believed in a God but were struggling to accept the strict laws and rules imposed by the Bible and their religion. I told them how important it was to question everything and decide for themselves what to believe.

Hoping to get some insights from these intelligent and open-minded men, I decided to show them the strange object I had found around Walden Pond. I had brought it on my recent camp trip at Follansbee Pond and had Dr. Agassiz examine it. Dr. Agassiz said it was just a strange rock that looked like it came from a volcanic eruption. When I mentioned it looked nothing like the other rocks found around the pond, he said the rock could have been carried by glaciers from someplace else and dropped in the area once the glaciers retreated. This made sense to me, and Dr. Agassiz was an expert in glaciers, but something still did not seem right.

So, I pulled the object out of my luggage and passed it around to the farmers. One of the farmers, Jefferson, said he had a brother who worked in the iron ore mine in Moriah and said I should bring it to him on my way home. He said he would take me to him tomorrow.

"Is there any more?" Ingrid asked. She tested to see if the last page of the journal was stuck to another page.

"That's the end of the journal," Jasper replied. "Are there any more journals?"

"Yes," Ingrid replied "But nothing that directly follows the date of that journal. His next journal chronologically starts with him back in Massachusetts."

"Well, shit," Jasper said.

"At least we know the object is real," Ingrid said. "And we know it was at John Brown's farm."

"That's outside of Lake Placid, right?" Jasper said.

"Yes. It's south of Lake Placid. I think it's a state historic site and used to be a National historic landmark before the Great Secession. I think they allow public access."

"Well, it's better than nothing," Jasper said, stifling a yawn.

"Let's get to bed and drive over there in the morning. It's only a half hour drive," Ingrid said.

"So, where do you have me sleeping?" Jasper asked.

"There's an empty dorm next to my apartment you can have for tonight. No TV but there is internet access."

"Thank God. I can't go one night without porn," Jasper joked.

"Well, you're not getting lucky tonight, so do whatever you have to do to be focused tomorrow," Ingrid said with a wry smile.

Ingrid walked Jasper to the dorm, and quickly showed him around, and then gave Jasper a hug goodnight. The minute Jasper's head hit the pillow, he was out cold.

CHAPTER 13

"The religion of one age is the literary entertainment of the next."

~ Ralph Waldo Emerson

ATLANTA, GA – OCTOBER 2035

Joel Robertson got out of bed and walked into the bathroom. As he took a leak he looked over the skyline of Atlanta from the top of the Atlanta Trump hotel. The typical smoggy haze covered most of the city, so he could see only a few blocks. Joel was sick of the haze. He was looking forward to getting his kids out of this muck and into his second home in the North Carolina mountains. Both his daughters had asthma that seemed to get worse every year. The government doctor said it was hereditary, but Joel was skeptical. He and wife did not have asthma and he wondered why it would get worse each year if it was hereditary.

"Joel, come back to bed," Tammy said from the bedroom.

Tammy was one of Joel's mistresses. Technically, she was a hooker because Joel paid her for her time. Tammy was married with kids, like Joel, but times were desperate in the Southern Republic, especially for African Americans. Tammy needed to feed and clothe her children, and prostitution still paid well. Although her husband was unhappy with the situation, he knew they needed the extra money she brought home.

Joel walked back into the bedroom and laid down next to Tammy on the bed.

"I didn't mean to wake you," Joel said, kissing Tammy's forehead.

"That's OK, I was up," Tammy replied. "When's your meeting?"

"In about half an hour," Joel replied. "But you can stay here as long as you want."

"Thank you. But I should leave too. I need to pick up my kids from school."

"How are your kids?" Joel asked. He got up from the bed and slid on his boxers.

"Much better since they've been at the Atlanta Evangelical High School. Shawn is thriving in his religious classes and Tina loves the music department. Thank you so much for getting them into that school. Their previous public high school was awful. There were shootings every month and teachers were constantly walking off the job due to low pay and lack of benefits. Some of their classes had over fifty students in them."

"I'm glad they're doing well. I heard Shawn is a pretty good basketball player. My kids love that high school as well." Joel slid on his dress pants. Most of the kids at the high school were from the surrounding gated communities. However, a few students from outside those communities were allowed in each year to show some diversity and improve their sports teams. It was not hard to get Shawn in to the school, but Joel had to pull some strings and grease some palms to get Tina in.

"Why can't you just make the public schools better?" Tammy asked as she got out of bed and put on her panties.

Joel scowled. He had told Tammy multiple times that she could not talk about politics with him. She should feel grateful for what she had. That's the problem with blacks,

Joel thought. They're never satisfied. You give them an inch and they want a mile. They need to know their place.

"I would love to, but we don't have the money for it," Joel replied. "Do you want higher taxes? Because that's the only way we can pay for it."

"Couldn't you take some money from your defense spending or your immigration police? Not many people are trying to cross the border anymore."

Joel turned his head to Tammy as he buttoned his dress shirt. "How dare you mention taking money from our men and women in uniform? They put their lives on the line every day while you and your husband take money from the government."

"I didn't mean that." Tammy fumbled for her shirt in the bed covers. "I just meant maybe the rich could pay..."

"I told you not to talk to me about politics," Joel yelled.

Suddenly there was a knock on the door of the hotel room.

"Sir, sorry to disturb you but it's time for the meeting," a voice called from outside.

"I'll be right out," Joel said.

"I'm so sorry Joel. It's not my place to question you," Tammy said. A tear ran down her face.

"The Secret Service will show you out. An agent will be waiting for you outside the door when you leave," Joel said.

Joel snatched his briefcase from the couch, opened the hotel room door, and then slammed it behind him. All minorities are the same, Joel thought as he followed the Secret Service agent down the hallway to the elevators. They all want to be treated special and have things given to them. And when they don't get them, they get violent. Like the illegal immigrant who killed his father in a fight. Joel was only ten at the time, but forty years later the image of the Mexican man standing over his father's lifeless body after slamming his head onto the concrete floor haunted him every day.

The United States had been formed as a white, Christian nation, Joel thought. The Southern Republic and the Texas Republic were the only republics that seemed to follow that. Joel believed that anyone besides white Christians were only guests in their republic. They would be allowed to stay, but they must know their place. You would not start taking food from a host's refrigerator if you were a guest in their house. You would not have sex with a host's daughter if you were a guest in their house. The homeowner has the ultimate say in what goes on their house. And if the homeowner feels that house is being threatened, they have the right to stop that threat. And stop it with deadly force if necessary.

The elevator door opened at the penthouse suite on the top of the Trump Hotel. Although most meetings were at the Southern White House in downtown Atlanta, President Donald Trump Jr. liked to have some meetings in his hotel. The government would foot the bill for the rooms and food, which would put a little extra money in Donald's pocket. Not that he needed any more of it. His family was by far the richest family in the Southern Republic.

Joel tried to push the conversation with Tammy out of his mind and mentally prepare for the cabinet meeting. Things were not going well, and he did not want to see the legendary Trump tantrum directed at him today.

As Joel walked into the room, he was upset to notice he was the last cabinet member to arrive. All the Trump family presidents had slashed cabinet level departments until there were only six departments left. The Department of Defense, Department of Treasury, Department of Commerce, Department of Agriculture, Department of Homeland Security, and Joel's Department of Religion.

As Joel sat down, President Trump entered the conference room. As they all stood up, Joel watched the president slowly stride into the room. Although in his late fifties, President Donald Trump Jr. had so many plastic surgery procedures it was difficult to determine his age. His formerly weak jawline was now well defined, he had somehow gained two inches in height, and there were no wrinkles on his fake tanned face.

After President Trump sat down, he distractedly waved his hand for the cabinet members to sit down as well.

"Alright, let's get this over with," President Trump said. "Jim, let's start with you."

James Covins was a former FBI agent and was now the head of Homeland Security. Before the secession, Jim had been fired from the FBI for investigating, arresting, and harassing members of left-wing activist groups. Joel knew Jim was a Catholic before he joined the Southern Republic. Like all major political figures in the Southern Republic, he was now a member of one of the official Evangelical and Prosperity faiths of the Southern Republic. But Joel had rarely seen Jim attend services. Joel was positive that Jim was still a Catholic at heart and hated him for it. Joel had assigned staff to look for dirt on Jim that Joel could use against him, but they had not come up with anything yet.

"Thank you, Mr. President," Jim said. He looked over his notes. "This month we've been very successful in arresting many members of socialist organizations plotting against the government. Just over the past few weeks we've arrested a hundred members of the Sierra Club, fifty members of Greenpeace, and twenty-five members of the ACLU."

"Very good, Jim," President Trump responded. "But who is financing these terrorist organizations?"

"We believe some of money has been coming from the Christian Democratic party, but we haven't been able to prove that yet. We also believe much of the money has come from other Republics, especially the Northeast and Pacific Republics."

"What's your plan to stop the flow of money to these terrorists?" President Trump asked as he took a sip of his coffee.

"I would like to request more money for my department to hire more customs agents along our northern border and at our airports. We currently do not have enough manpower to capture terrorists from the other republics infiltering our society and funding these terrorist organizations."

"Bullshit," Joel thought as he pretended to look down at his notes. The Department of Homeland Security was flush with money. And he knew that any additional funds would mostly end up in Jim's hands anyway. His four mansions were not being paid for through his official government salary.

"I also would like to request permission to bug the offices of the Christian Democratic Party. That's the only way we can know which members of Congress are supporting these radical organizations," Jim added.

"Consider it done," President Trump replied. "Now Frank, what are you doing about the stock market?"

As the Commerce Secretary, Frank Desick, droned on about corporate bailouts and subsidies, Joel quickly lost interest. It was the fault of the other republics and Mexico that things were not going well in the Southern Republic, he thought. Their sanctions and trickery were destroying this moral and godly republic they had built. It filled Joel with intense rage when he thought about it. Why wouldn't the whites in the other republics realize that they should be the only rulers of this former country, rather than the hordes of unwashed masses who caused the secession?

"Joel," President Trump said. "How goes it in the churches?"

Joel, a bit startled, rummaged through his papers. "Very good, sir. Donations to the churches have mostly recovered from the dip we saw last quarter." Joel knew this was bullshit, but he knew he would be fired if he kept giving the president bad news.

"The new tithing law coming into effect this month should make the monthly donations return to their former levels," Joel added. "Also, we should get some more converts after taxes are raised on all the unofficial churches this year."

"I've heard rumors about some sort of potential artifact in the Northeast Republic. Are you on top of that?" President Trump asked.

"Fucking Billy," Joel thought as he flipped through his notes. He had forgotten Billy was close with Donald's brother Eric. Those two idiots loved each other's company.

"I'm on top of it," Joel said. "You have nothing to worry about."

CHAPTER 14

"I, John Brown, am now quite certain that the crimes of this guilty land can never be purged away but with blood. I had, as I now think, vainly flattered myself that without very much bloodshed, it might be done."

~ John Brown (Written on a note that John Brown handed to the guard at his execution)

LAKE PLACID, NY – OCTOBER 2035

After a quick breakfast in the cafeteria, Ingrid and Jasper got in Jasper's car and started the thirty-minute drive to the John Brown Farm State Historical Site. They took a left turn at the sign for the site off Route 73 and headed down the dirt road. At the end of the road, the dense forest opened into a large field. The site consisted of one large house, one small house, a barn, a statue, and a fenced-in graveyard.

Jasper parked the Trybrid in a small dirt parking lot and got out of the car. It was a beautiful fall morning and the views from the open field were spectacular. In this high peak part of the Adirondack Park, fall colors were at full peak. Yellows, reds, and greens dotted the sides of Whiteface Mountain to the north and the high peaks of Algonquin Peak and Mount Marcy to the south. Fallen leaves blanketed the dirt road and field with a carpet of stunning colors. Lately, Jasper was trying to be more present and appreciate each moment instead of ruminating about the past or worrying about the future. Jasper had been failing in the last few days, but the beauty and peace of the morning enabled him briefly to feel a little bit of bliss.

The Lake Placid Olympic Ski Jumping Complex, comprised of 90-meter and 120-meter ski jumps built for the 1980 Winter Olympics, was an imposing sight in front of the Adirondack peaks. Lake Placid hosted the Winter Olympics in 1932 and 1980 and was especially renowned as the site of the 1980 USA–USSR hockey game. Dubbed the "Miracle on Ice", a group of American college students and amateurs upset the heavily favored Soviet national ice hockey team 4–3, and two days later won the gold medal.

Jasper recalled his parents taking him and his brother on a tour of the ski jumps. They had taken the elevator to the top of the 120-meter jump, where an enclosed glass room allowed amazing views of the surrounding area and the scary view the skiers had as they started their jumps. Although it was autumn now, summer ski jumping training was likely still in session. From his tour of the ski jumps with his parents, Jasper remembered a display that described the history of the ski jumps. In the olden days, summer ski jumping used to be on snow, because blocks of ice were removed from area lakes and stored until needed for the competitions. This ice was brought to the jumps and crushed into the hill. Crews laboriously spread this "snow" along the length of the site to allow the event to occur. However, artificial surfaces, introduced in Europe for summer training, eventually made their way to Lake Placid. Now the in-run, where the jumpers gain speed, is made of porcelain tile troughs, while the landing hill is a synthetic surface layered like a thatched roof. When the in-run and the landing hill are watered, the result is a winter replica of speeds and jumping distance.

"So, what are we looking for here?" Ingrid asked.

"Not sure," Jasper replied as they walked toward the small information center. "Let's look around, talk to the people who work here, and see if we can find anything that can help us."

"Hello, welcome to John Brown's farm. My name is Ellen," the older woman behind the welcome desk at the visitor center said.

"Hi," Jasper replied as he walked over to the desk. "We would like to tour the grounds and perhaps talk to a historian if one is available."

"Great," Ellen said. "I'm the onsite historian and I'm leading a general tour in about fifteen minutes. I would be happy to talk to you and answer any questions you may have after the tour. Cost is ten dollars a person."

"Sounds perfect," Jasper replied. He handed Ellen a twenty-dollar bill.

After taking a short walk around the site, Jasper and Ingrid returned to the visitor center, where Ellen stood in the center of a group of six people. There was an elderly couple, a family with a husband, wife, and two bored teenagers, and a forty something single man with balding blond hair and a beer belly. As they approached the group, Ellen started her spiel.

"Welcome to the John Brown State Historical Site. Our tour will include an inside look at John Brown's farmhouse and barn, as well as the caretaker's house. We'll also visit the statue of John Brown and finally the family graveyard. Please follow me, we'll start with the house."

The house was a two and a half story timber framed structure with a gable roof and clapboarded exterior. Its front was four bays wide, with the entrance in the left center bay topped by a transom window.

The tour followed Ellen into the entrance and they all stopped in the main room of the house.

"In 1848, Brown heard of Gerrit Smith's Adirondack land grants to poor black men and decided to move his family among the new settlers," Ellen said. "He and his sons bought the land we're standing on for one dollar an acre and they built the house we're standing in now. In 1855, Brown moved to Kansas to support his sons' efforts to keep Kansas a free-state under the popular sovereignty laws, leaving his wife and several of his children behind. Brown returned to visit his family here several times. After he was executed, his wife returned his body here for burial. The family sold the property, except for the graveyard, in 1863. In 1870 it was purchased by journalist Kate Field, who formed an association to oversee its preservation and make it accessible to visitors. It was acquired by the State of New York in 1896 as a National Historic Landmark before the Great Secession."

They continued the tour of the house, and then went through the farmhouse and the caretaker's house. All were the original buildings whose exteriors and interiors had been restored to match their assumed mid-1800s appearance.

Stepping outside of the caretaker's house, the tour group followed Ellen to the statue. The statue was a fifteen-foot bronze statue constructed by Joseph Pollia. The statue was a larger than life representation of John Brown with his hand around the shoulders of an African-American youth. The youth was looking up at John while trying to keep his tattered clothes from falling off his shoulder. The bearded John Brown, who did not seem to have the beard often seen in other photographs, looked down at the young African-American boy. As the tour group admired the statue, Ellen gave a detailed description of John Brown's life.

"John Brown was an American abolitionist who believed in and advocated armed insurrection as the only way to overthrow the institution of slavery in the United States. He first gained attention when he led small groups of volunteers during the Bleeding Kansas crisis of 1856. Dissatisfied with the pacifism of the organized abolitionist movement, Brown and his supporters killed five supporters of slavery in the Pottawatomie massacre, which responded to the sacking of Lawrence by pro-slavery forces. Brown then commanded anti-slavery forces at the Battle of Black Jack and the Battle of Osawatomie."

Ellen continued, "In 1859, Brown led a raid on the federal armory at Harpers Ferry to start a liberation movement among the slaves there. During the raid, he seized the armory; seven people were killed, and ten or more were injured. He intended to arm slaves with weapons from the arsenal, but the attack failed. Within thirty-six hours, Brown's men had fled or been killed or captured by local pro-slavery farmers, militiamen, and US Marines led by Robert E. Lee. The Commonwealth of Virginia tried John Brown for treason, the murder of five men, and inciting a slave insurrection. Brown was found guilty on all counts and hanged."

"The Harpers Ferry raid escalated tensions that, a year later, led to the South's secession and the Civil War. Brown's raid captured the nation's attention, as Southerners feared it was the first of many Northern plots to cause a slave rebellion that might endanger their lives. 'John Brown's Body' was a popular Union marching song during the Civil War and portrayed Brown as a martyr," said Ellen.

"Some people believe he was a madman and terrorist!"

A quiet gasp escaped the tour group as they all turned to look at the balding blond man who had made the comment.

"That is true," Ellen said, quickly composing herself. "Some historians have compared him to Osama bin Laden and Timothy McVeigh, but most historians argue that he lived in very violent times and although some of his tactics were extreme, his ideas were pure and ahead of his time."

"Didn't he kill a slave?" the man asked. Discomfort in the rest of the group started to become evident.

"His raiding party did kill a railroad baggage handler, who ironically was a free black, when he refused their orders to halt," Ellen stated, keeping remarkably cool and composed. "However, John Brown did not personally kill that man. In fact, during that same raid, he spared the lives of many people. He spared the lives of the wife and teenage son of one of the men they killed, even though these people could have identified the raiders. At another cabin, he interrogated two men and let them go, convinced they had not threatened free state settlers or been involved in violent actions against the free state settlers."

An eerie silence fell over the site after Ellen finished her response. History could be a messy affair, Jasper thought. Every historical movie or book attempts to portray a true villain versus a true hero, but real people are not easily placed in those categories. If you believe slavery was an abomination and a terrible injustice, John Brown's actions would be justified. If you believed that slavery was only an unfortunate period of US history, John Brown's actions would be cruel and extreme.

"Thank you for that information," the balding man finally said. He smiled broadly.

"You're welcome," said Ellen. "Let us all continue to the gravesite."

The tour group followed Ellen as she slowly walked to the small family cemetery.

"After John Brown was captured at Harpers Ferry, he was charged with murdering four whites and a black, conspiring with slaves to rebel, and treason against Virginia. After a week-long trial and forty-five minutes of deliberation, the jury found Brown guilty on all three counts and Brown was sentenced to be hanged in public. In response to the sentence, Ralph Waldo Emerson remarked that John 'will make the gallows glorious like the Cross.'

"Brown refused to be rescued by Silas Soule, a friend from Kansas who had somehow infiltrated the Jefferson County Jail and offered to break him out during the night and flee northward. Brown supposedly told Silas that he was too old to live a life on the run from the federal authorities and was ready to die as a martyr. Silas left him behind to be executed. More importantly, many of Brown's letters exuded high tones of spirituality and conviction and, when picked up by the northern press, won increasing numbers of supporters in the North as they simultaneously infuriated many white people in the South.

"On the morning of his execution, John read his Bible and wrote a final letter to his wife, which included his will. At 11:00 a.m. he was escorted from the county jail through a crowd of two thousand soldiers, to a small field a few blocks ıway where the gallows were. Among the soldiers in the rowd were future Confederate General Stonewall Jackson ıd John Wilkes Booth, who had borrowed a militia uni- ·m to gain admission to the execution.

"Brown was accompanied by the sheriff and his assista s, but no minister since he had consistently rejected the mı strations of pro-slavery clergy. He elected to receive no reli ›us services in the jail or at the scaffold. He was hanged at 1 '5 a.m. and pronounced dead at 11:50 a.m. His body was ı .ced in a wooden coffin with the noose still around his neck. His coffin was then put on a train to take it from Virginia to this family cemetery where he is now buried."

A long moment of silence fell over the group. Finally, after a respectful minute, Ellen spoke. "Thank you for coming on the tour, I'll be happy to answer any questions you may have."

As the rest of tour group slowly wandered away, Ingrid and Jasper walked up to Ellen.

"Do you have any archival information on John Brown or the farm?" Jasper asked Ellen.

"Yes, we have a small archive in the back of the visitor center," Ellen said. "We usually only allow access by appointment from a university or a historical society."

"I understand, but I'm an archeologist of the Northeast Republic," Jasper said, handing her his government ID. "I was wondering if you could do us a favor and let us take a quick look in your archive today?"

"I guess so," Ellen said as she gave Jasper back his ID card. "But I can only give you a couple hours. I can't let anyone in the archives without being on-site myself."

"That would be fine," Jasper said. "We really appreciate it."

"Follow me." Ellen said as she walked back to the visitor center.

Entering the visitor center, Jasper and Ingrid followed Ellen behind the front desk and through a door in the back. The door opened into a small room about the size of a normal business office.

"The archives are organized by year as labeled on the shelves," Ellen said, pointing across the room. "Please put everything back exactly as you found it. You are free to make copies at the copy machine outside. Please just keep track of the number of pages you copy. We will charge you five cents a page. Please only take out small amounts of the archives at a time as this room is climate controlled while the visitor center is not. If you have any questions, please come see me. I will be either in the visitor center or out leading a tour."

"Thank you so much Ellen," Jasper said. "We will be careful."

"No problem. You have about four hours," Ellen said. She checked her watch and closed the door behind her.

"Okay, what are we looking for here?" Ingrid asked as she started perusing the stacks on the shelves.

"I think any journals or diaries from either John Brown, his family, or any of the black farmers who owned land around here. How about you take that shelf and I'll take this one?" Jasper said, pointing to shelves on each side of the room.

"Sounds good."

As they went through the archives and writings of John Brown, Jasper was amazed at what an incredible man he was. Jasper thought he knew who he was, but John Brown was a very complex man. Brown's actions as an abolitionist, and the tactics he chose, made him a controversial figure. Jasper thought he should be memorialized as a heroic martyr and a visionary, but even some of his anti-slavery allies did not condone his actions. However, Jasper was finding nothing on any weird object that Emerson brought to the farm. He assumed Ingrid was not finding anything either.

"Sorry, but we're locking things up now," Ellen said, opening the door. "Did you find what you were looking for?"

"No," Jasper said. "But we really appreciate you allowing us the access to your archives."

"My pleasure," Ellen said. Jasper and Ingrid followed Ellen outside as she locked the door to the visitor center and set the alarm. It was late afternoon and it was looking like a beautiful sunset.

"Is it okay if we walk around here outside for a while?" Jasper asked Ellen.

"Of course," Ellen said. "Have a good night."

"You too," Ingrid and Jasper said at the same time.

As they watched Ellen drive away down the dirt road, Ingrid and Jasper walked over to the cemetery and paused over John Brown's headstone.

"What do you think of John Brown?" Ingrid asked. She turned her head from the headstone and faced toward Jasper.

"He was an amazing man," Jasper said. "He was ahead of his time in seeing that the only way slavery was going to end was through bloodshed."

"He was a terrorist!"

Ingrid and Jasper turned around to see the balding man who was with the tour group, along with two more men. These new men were tall and heavy like the man on the tour, but more muscular, with tattoos covering their necks and exposed arms. The two larger men both held handguns that were directed toward Ingrid and Jasper.

"Who are you?" Jasper asked.

"My name is Billy, and these are my associates John and Mark." the man said, pointing to the two large men with guns on each side of him. "How's the research going?"

"What research?"

"You're a terrible liar, just like your friend Riley," Billy said.

"What have you done with Riley?" Jasper asked. He began to approach Billy.

Having lost control of his emotions and caution with the mention of Riley, Jasper did not notice Mark come up alongside him until he struck him on the head with the butt of his revolver.

"Fuck!" Jasper screamed, reaching for his head. He fell to one knee as the pain rushed through him.

"Your friend Riley is fine," Billy said. "You two, however, will not be. My boss said to follow you if you were making progress, but you seem to be wasting time doing historical research. So, unless you can tell me the location of the artifact, these two gentlemen are going to kill you."

"We aren't going to tell you anything until you let Riley go," Ingrid said.

"We're not going to let Riley go," Billy replied. "He knows way too much about the artifact and we've made more progress with his information than you two have. Therefore, you're both expendable. Let's go."

Billy waved his hands at his two henchmen, and they all started down a hiking trail adjacent to the historical site. The henchmen pushed Ingrid and Jasper in this direction, with John behind Jasper, and Mark behind Ingrid. They all walked down the trail in silence. Jasper thought about screaming bloody murder at the top of his lungs, but no one was around. The site had cleared out, and Jasper tried to formulate some sort of plan before he and Ingrid got shot in the back of the head in the middle of the woods.

Just as Jasper was finalizing some stupid plan of attack based off a movie he saw once, the forest opened to the base of the ski jumps. Nobody was around as Billy broke open the door at the base of the higher 120-meter ski jump with a crowbar.

His curiosity piqued, Jasper temporarily forgot about his shitty plan and asked, "Where are we going?"

"To the top of the ski jump," Billy said. "We need to make this look like an accident. The police are already looking for Riley, so we don't want them to have anything to link your murder with his kidnapping."

The henchmen shoved Ingrid and Jasper into the building and they all crammed into the elevator. An uncomfortable silence came over the car as Ingrid and Jasper waited to die and the henchmen waited to kill them. Jasper grasped Ingrid's hand and looked into her eyes. Jasper had really missed her and had loved their recent time together. He wanted to tell Ingrid all this, but all he could get out was a weak smile.

Finally, the elevator doors opened, and Ingrid and Jasper were shoved into the observation booth. Billy walked over to the door leading out into the jump and used the crowbar to break it open.

"Ladies first," Billy said as he pointed at Ingrid. Jasper looked at Ingrid, and Mark gave her a shove toward the door. Her hand broke away from Jasper's and he looked at her face. She quietly mouthed "it's okay" as she passed Jasper toward the door.

It was not okay. Ingrid's calmness and bravery jolted Jasper out of his despondency. He decided that he would not go meekly, and he would rather be shot than fall two hundred feet to his death. Jasper quickly swung his body around and grabbed John's hands behind him. John was bigger and stronger than Jasper, but Jasper had surprised him enough that he was able to push John's hands and his gun straight up over their heads. A shot discharged from the revolver and went through the ceiling. Jasper's ears rang in pain at the noise, but he maintained his concentration and threw his right leg forward with as much power as he could muster, right into John's groin.

It was a direct hit and John keeled over, screaming in pain. As he keeled over, Jasper wrestled the revolver from his hands and it fell to the floor. Jasper quickly kicked the gun away from John and turned around to see Ingrid struggling with Mark. They both had their hands on his gun. Ingrid had forced the direction of the gun off to the side of her, but the much stronger Mark was slowly pushing its aim back at Ingrid.

Mark had his back to Jasper as he ran toward him and laid the full force of his shoulder into the center of Mark's back. Ingrid had seen Jasper coming, so as Mark fell forward from the blow to his back, Ingrid jumped out of the way and helped push him through the door. With his momentum, Mark fell over the railing on the overlook outside and plummeted to the ground below.

As Jasper turned toward Billy, he saw a movement out of the corner of his eye and ducked as fast as he could. Billy's wild swing of his crowbar barely missed the top of Jasper's head. As Jasper climbed to his feet, Ingrid moved toward Billy after his missed swing left him vulnerable and kicked him right in the groin. Billy fell to the ground screaming in pain and dropped the crowbar to the ground. As Ingrid picked up the crowbar, Jasper turned back toward John, the henchman he had kicked in the crotch. John had just grabbed the gun that had dropped to the floor and was starting to raise it toward Ingrid and Jasper.

Jasper clutched Ingrid and they both sprinted out the door onto the ski jump outside. They heard the gun discharge and Jasper turned around and looked through the window to see John struggling to aim. He still could not stand up straight, but was stumbling, hunched over, toward the door. Jasper took Ingrid by her hand and dragged her onto the steps next to the ski jump.

"What are you doing?" she said.

"Trying to save our asses," Jasper answered. "Jump on the ramp!"

Ingrid and Jasper jumped on the ski jump ramp, landing on their butts. As another bullet zinged past their heads, they started sliding down the ramp. There was no snow on the ramp, but the material used for the summer jumpers was very slick and they quickly picked up speed.

"Grab my leg," Jasper yelled to Ingrid, who was sliding in front of him. Once Ingrid turned around and clutched

Jasper's leg, Jasper started dragging his hands and feet to slow them down. Jasper was able to slow them down a little, but they were still going to slide off the end of the ski jump if they didn't think of something else soon.

As they hit the flatter part of the jump, Jasper noticed a post at the end of the jump along the side. "Hold on tight to my leg," Jasper yelled to Ingrid. He reached over with his left hand as far as he could stretch. Jasper's hand just caught the post on the edge of ramp and he grabbed onto it for dear life. Jasper's legs and Ingrid's body swung over the edge of the ramp as Jasper was barely able to hold his grip on the post. Once their swinging back and forth finally settled, Jasper grasped the post with both hands, but his grip was slipping.

"Can you grab onto anything?" Jasper yelled to Ingrid.

"Yes!" Ingrid said. She reached over and grasped the scaffolding underneath the edge of the jump. Slowly Ingrid released her hand from Jasper's leg and she climbed completely onto a platform. Jasper reached for the scaffold underneath him, and they both slowly climbed down to the ground.

"You okay?" Jasper asked, trying to catch his breath, once they were finally on the ground.

"Yes, how about you?" Ingrid said, looking around.

"I'm fine," Jasper said. He looked up at the thirty stories they just slid down. "Let's go, I think in their condition we can beat them to the car."

Ingrid and Jasper sprinted through the woods and reached the car, which was still parked in the dirt parking lot. Jasper started it up, peeled out of the parking lot, shot down the dirt road, and turned left onto the highway. Jasper looked in the rearview mirror and slowed down once he was convinced they were not being followed.

"Should we call 911?" Ingrid said.

"From what phone?" Jasper said. "I know we can make it anonymous, but if we call from one of our cell phones I'm sure they'll be able to trace the call."

"I guess so," Ingrid said. "It seems wrong to leave the scene and not notify anyone. Do you think we should consider calling the police and explain to them what happened?"

"That's an option," Jasper replied. "But we both know what would happen. We would waste days making statements and being interviewed. Although we were just acting in self-defense, both of us are alive while that one guy is dead. That does not look good. Plus, we don't know how connected those guys are. They could have allies in the police force that could keep us in jail or try to kill us again."

"You're right," Ingrid said. "Where do we go now?"

"Well, I don't think Serenity Village is safe for us to go, they probably followed us from there. Perhaps we should find a hotel in Lake Placid. There are a bunch of hotels and we should be able to blend in with the tourists."

"That makes sense, but we're getting separate rooms."

"Separate rooms!" Jasper said. "We just went through a traumatic experience together. Aren't we supposed to bond over that and have a night of hot sex in a strange hotel room?"

Ingrid laughed. "You've changed. I remember when we first started going out back in grad school I had to make the first move because I thought you were never going to make it. I want us to be together when we're ready, not only because we had a traumatic experience together."

"Okay," Jasper said. "Let's find someplace to stay."

As they drove into Lake Placid, Jasper realized the only place he knew of there was the High Peaks Lodge at the end of the downtown strip. His brother had his marriage reception there about twenty years ago. Jasper remember it being a nice place, so they stopped there first.

They had two rooms available that were next door to each other. They were a bit pricey, but they had a large parking lot that they could hide the car in. Also, Jasper thought that the more they drove around the greater the chance someone would spot his car.

After throwing their stuff into the rooms, they headed down to the Three Bears Lounge in the hotel for something to eat.

"We're both pretty dirty fighters," Jasper said after they ordered their food. "Both of us went for the groin right away."

Ingrid and Jasper laughed. It felt good to release a bit of the tension.

"Whatever works," Ingrid said. "All those guys were huge, so I don't think either of us had much of a choice."

"Agreed," Jasper said.

"So, what do we do now?" Ingrid asked. She took a sip of her iced tea.

"Well, John Brown's farm seems to have been a dead end," Jasper replied. "Plus, it's not safe to go back there anyway."

"Didn't Emerson's journal say that one of the black farmers was going to take him to see his brother who worked on the mine in Moriah?" Ingrid said.

"Yes, I think it did."

"There's an Iron Center Museum and historical society in Moriah," Ingrid said. "There's a chance something is there."

"Well, it's better than nothing," Jasper said as their poutine appetizer arrived.

"Let's drive over there in the morning. It's only a half hour drive," Ingrid dug into the gooey mix of fries, gravy, and cheese curds with her fork.

"Sounds like a plan," Jasper said.

Jasper and Ingrid finished their meal and walked back to their adjoining rooms.

"No chance for a nightcap, I assume?" Jasper asked, smiling at Ingrid as she unlocked her door.

Ingrid smiled back. "Sorry, I'm exhausted and I know you are too. Sleep well." She gave Jasper a quick peck on the lips and went into her room.

Ingrid was right, Jasper thought, he was exhausted. Jasper got in the room, fell on the bed, and was out cold.

Chapter 15

"Shallow men believe in luck or in circumstance.
Strong men believe in cause and effect."

~ Ralph Waldo Emerson

Moriah, NY - August 1858

Ralph, Jefferson, and Jefferson's brother Moses scraped up the last morsels of their dinner. Even though it was only rice and beans, it was very nourishing after a long day of horseback riding from North Elba to outside the mining settlement of Moriah. Moses had built a beautiful fire outside his tent and they all enjoyed some whiskey Moses had purchased in the company store.

"Mr. Emerson," Jefferson said. "Would you like to show Moses the rock you showed me last night?"

"I would," Ralph said as he pulled the object from his rucksack. "But I would like to share with you what happened to me late last night after you went to bed Jefferson, if that's okay. I think it may shed some additional light on what this object may be."

"Of course, Mr. Emerson," Jefferson replied. Moses nodded in agreement.

"Thank you," Ralph replied. "Before heading to bed last night, I took a walk around the farm. The object is extremely light, so I took it with me. The moon was full, and it was relatively easy to find my way among the fields and the cabins of the farm. I decided to sit down on a tree stump.

"Sitting on the stump I looked up at the moon and wondered if humans would ever visit the moon or the planets. What a wonder it would be to travel across space and explore new worlds. How much we could learn about ourselves and our relationship with this world by travelling around the universe. As I sat there, I held the object and ran my hand over its surface. It was so smooth and so white, it boggled my mind as to what it could be. I am not a geologist, so I had to defer to Dr. Agassiz's theory that it was a rock dropped by the receding glaciers thousands of years ago. I deeply respect Dr. Agassiz's expertise, but something about his theory does not sit quite right with me. As I placed my hand on the flat side of the object, it lit up like it had a candle inside it. I took a closer look at the object and..."

"Well, what do we have here?" A voice from the woods surprised the group in the night. Three men appeared from the woods. Each had a long, heavy beard, dusty, worn clothes, and carried a wooden club.

"Looks like two negroes and a highfalutin nancy," answered one of the men.

"Why don't you join us?" Ralph said, trying to diffuse the situation. He stood up and got a measure of the men surrounding them. Ralph assumed they were local miners due to their strong arms and their dusty clothes. They all had a strong odor of alcohol.

"Do you have any whiskey?" said one of the men. He appeared to be the youngest of their group.

"Yes, we do," Ralph offered.

"Do you have any money?" an older man asked, the one who had called out initially.

“Why do you ask?” Ralph said, still trying to diffuse the situation. Ralph looked over at Jefferson and Moses, who were silent and obviously very nervous about these newcomers. Ralph was nervous too, but he hoped he could talk the men out of doing something evil.

Suddenly, the younger man landed a sharp blow to Jefferson’s face with his club. “Where is your money, boy?” he screamed as Jefferson clutched at his bleeding mouth.

Filled with rage, Ralph bolted over to the younger man and threw his body at him. They both fell to the ground hard. Their fall to the ground released the younger man’s grip on the club and Ralph climbed on top of him. Ralph laid hard blows to the man’s face until he felt a sharp blow to the back of his head. Everything went dark.

~ ~ ~

“Mr. Emerson, are you all right?”

Struggling to focus on the sound of the voice, Ralph slowly opened his eyes to see Jefferson and Moses hovering over him.

“My head hurts,” Ralph said weakly. The back right of his skull pounded in pain as he tried to get up.

“Please Mr. Emerson, stay down. You took quite a blow,” Moses said as he put a blanket underneath Ralph’s head.

Coming to his senses, Ralph was finally able to focus on Jefferson and Moses. Jefferson had dried blood caked to the left side of his mouth and Moses had a large bruise on his right cheek and a black eye.

“Oh, my goodness,” Ralph said. “Are you both alright?”

“Yes, Mr. Emerson, nothing worse than what has happened to us before.”

“What happened?” Ralph asked.

"As you were punching the younger man on the ground, the older man clubbed you in the back of the head," Jefferson said. "You went out cold and Moses jumped up after the older man and caught him with a good punch to the head. The man went down but the third man caught Moses in the face with his club and Moses went down as well. I'm sorry I could not have helped more, but that boy caught me on the mouth pretty hard."

"There was nothing you could have done, Jefferson," Moses said. "After getting me on the ground, those boys sobered up a bit after seeing that they knocked out a white man. They quickly grabbed up all the money and loot they could easily get and ran off into the woods."

"Did you get a good look at them, so we can report them to the sheriff?" Ralph asked.

"Wouldn't do any good," Moses replied. "Those boys work at the mines and the sheriff is paid by the mines. They won't punish them from the story of two negroes and one outsider."

"What did they get?" Ralph asked, finally getting himself to a sitting position.

"They got my stove, some money from all of us, and your watch," Jefferson said.

"Did they get the object I brought?" Ralph asked, frantically looking around the fire.

"They did, Mr. Emerson," Jefferson said. "I'm so sorry."

CHAPTER 16

"Finish each day and be done with it. You have done what you could. Some blunders and absurdities no doubt crept in; forget them as soon as you can. Tomorrow is a new day. You shall begin it serenely and with too high a spirit to be encumbered with your old nonsense."

~ Ralph Waldo Emerson

LAKE PLACID, NY – OCTOBER 2035

Jasper woke up with a start to banging on his hotel door.

"Come on, Jasper, get up," Ingrid said as she continued to hammer on the door.

Jasper walked over to the door and flung it open.

"I'm up," Jasper said, groggy and a bit pissed off. "The adjoining door was unlocked, why didn't you come in and wake me like a normal person?"

"I didn't know what you could be doing in here and I didn't want to find out."

"Come on, you know I'm not a morning person," Jasper said.

"Good," Ingrid said. "Now get dressed and meet me at breakfast."

Jasper got dressed and went down to the hotel restaurant, where they had a buffet breakfast. Jasper served himself some oatmeal and a coffee and sat down across from Ingrid.

"You sleep okay?" Ingrid asked.

"I fell asleep quickly but woke up sweating after a mass of terrible dreams," Jasper replied.

"What type of dreams?" Ingrid asked.

"All types of dreams, but they all contained the vision of that man falling to his death off the ski jump," Jasper said. "And I'm still reliving that moment today in my head. Why did I kill him?"

"You didn't try to kill him," Ingrid grasped Jasper's hand across the table. "You were trying to save me. I also had bad dreams last night about that moment, but they were going to kill us. You had no choice."

"I know," Jasper replied. "But I've never seen anyone die in front of me like that. I didn't mean to kill him, but my blow caused him to fall. He was probably just earning a paycheck and he died from it. I can't seem to stop thinking about it."

"It's haunting me too," Ingrid said squeezing Jasper's hand. "But we have to put it behind us for right now and concentrate. Riley is counting on us."

"You're right," Jasper replied. "What's next?"

"So, I looked up the email of the woman who works at the Iron Museum in Moriah," Ingrid said as she released Jasper's hand and took a sip of her coffee. "I emailed her last night and she called me back this morning. The museum is not open to the public anymore due to budget cuts, but she said she would open it up for us and let us go through whatever historical documents and journals they have."

"That's great," Jasper said.

"There is a catch though."

"What is it?"

"We have to pretend we're married and both practicing Catholics."

"Why do we have to do that?" Jasper asked.

"Well, first she introduced herself as Sister Elizabeth. Then she said that the public is no longer allowed to view any of the historical documents unless they're specifically looking for information on their relatives. So, long story short, I told her we were married, and you were looking for information on one of your relatives."

"You lied to a nun?" Jasper said.

"I know, I feel terrible about it."

"And why did you say it was my relative we're looking for?" Jasper asked.

"Well, I don't think there were many Latinos working or living in Moriah back in the day," Ingrid said with a wry smile. "Plus, don't you have ancestors who lived in Moriah?"

"Yes, I can't believe you remember that," Jasper said. "My great, great, great granduncle was a priest in Moriah for a long time. So that part is true, but saying we're married and practicing Catholics is still a lie."

"Well, you could still be a practicing Catholic for all I know," Ingrid said. "I know you used to be and you could have returned to the church since I left the country."

"No. I have a lot of Catholic guilt, but not enough to go back to church. I especially hated going to confession." Jasper said. "Have I ever told you about the last time I went to confession?"

"I don't think so," Ingrid replied.

"Every month my mother made me confess my sins to a priest, and he would forgive those sins and 'sentence' me to a penance. The penance was usually only a few prayers or an action or apology you had to do."

"I know what penance and confession is," Ingrid replied. "My parents were atheists, but we grew up in a country that was ninety percent Catholic."

"Oh, yeah, I forgot. Anyway, my mother was more than happy to tell me what my sins were. My mother would say,

'You fought with your brother, you lied to me, and you talked back to your father.'

"So, I ended up using these sins as my go-to list even as I got older. The only thing I added to the list was impure thoughts. I thought as I hit puberty there was no way a priest was going to believe I didn't have at least some impure thoughts. But as I reached the end of high school, these thoughts started turning into actions. I was a late bloomer but believe me I made up for lost time. I even started to have something vaguely resembling sex. I was having orgasms all over the place, but my girlfriend, not so much. Since I was still a good Catholic boy, sort of, I felt guilty about it and decided to confess it.

"Scared as shit, I walked into the confession booth, knelt, and confessed my sins: 'Forgive me Father for I have sinned. Since my last confession I have fought with my brother, lied to my mother, talked back to my father, swore while playing video games, had impure thoughts, and performed impure actions.'"

"What did the priest say?" Ingrid asked.

"There was a brief pause and the priest said, 'Were these impure actions with yourself or someone else?'"

"What did you say?" Ingrid took another sip of her coffee

"Well, when you go to confession, the last thing you want is a follow up question or any type of conversation. Nothing good comes from it. You just want to get in there, get your sins forgiven, and go back to sinning. As I was eighteen at that time, I'd been doing plenty of impure actions with myself for quite some time, but that would have caused all sorts of questions. So, I replied, 'With someone else.'" He asked me how old I was, and I said eighteen. Then he asked, 'how old is she?' and I said, seventeen. There was a very long pause and the priest finally said, 'Alright, say five Our Fathers and ten Hail Marys, in the name of the Father, the Son, and the Holy Ghost. Amen.'"

"So, I guess having sex before marriage is not a mortal sin," Ingrid said.

"Not to that priest."

Ingrid and Jasper finished breakfast and drove the half hour to the Iron Museum. The museum was in an old brick building in the small village of Port Henry. The discovery and mining of iron in the Adirondacks caused a boom in the local economy of Port Henry in the 17th century. It also processed iron in smelting and shipped products from Port Henry on Lake Champlain. These operations were conducted from 1824 until 1971. After the mining and smelting ended, the local economy stagnated and slowly moved toward tourism.

Before the breakup of the US, the area was fortunate to have retirees and second homeowners to prop up local commerce, but the economy had regressed since the secessions and Port Henry had regressed as well. The only stores open that morning were a Stewarts and a marijuana dispensary.

Jasper and Ingrid parked in the empty parking lot of the museum and knocked on the front door. Opening the door was a sweet old woman with cat's eye glasses and curly grey hair.

"Hello, you must be Jasper and Ingrid," she said as she let them in. "My name is Sister Elizabeth, but you can call me Betty."

"Hi, Betty," Ingrid answered. "Thank you so much for letting us look through your museum and documents today."

"Of course, dear," Betty replied. Turning to Jasper she asked, "So Jasper, tell me about which relative you wanted to find information about."

"Well, one of my relatives, Clarence Brennan, was a priest during the mid-to-late 1800s. I would like to find information about him and the town during that time. Any information about visitors, strange happenings, or strange objects found during mining work are also of interest to me."

"Well, we have some old newspapers like the Elizabethtown Post and the Essex County Republican," Betty replied. "In addition, the mine put out its own company newspaper. That may have the information you're looking for."

"That sounds great, sister, thank you," Jasper replied.

"Please call me Betty."

Ingrid and Jasper spent the entire day looking through every newspaper in the museum. Lots of births, lots of deaths, lots of arrests for fighting, and even some murders. But there was nothing mentioning Emerson, or any strange object brought into town or discovered at the mine.

Betty helped them by bringing out the newspapers to the research table and asking if they needed anything. When she wasn't helping Ingrid and Jasper, Betty prayed with her rosary and read her Bible.

After the day was done, Jasper and Ingrid asked Betty out to dinner to repay her for her kindness. She happily accepted, and they went to the Inn at Westport. As they all started eating their burgers, Betty asked, "Why do you think so many Catholics are leaving the church?"

Jasper gave Ingrid the evil eye and said, "Well I think it has to do with how the Church treats women and homosexuals."

"The church has improved on that," Betty retorted.

"Yes, it has," Jasper admitted. "But they still don't allow women to be priests and ban practicing homosexuals from the church."

"The Bible says that women can't be priests and that homosexuals cannot be in the church," Betty said.

"The Bible says a lot of things," Jasper said. "It also says women must submit to their husbands and slaves must submit to their masters. I assume you don't agree with those passages."

"No, I don't," Betty replied. "I admit I have a lot of issues with how the church has been run since I joined. The pedophilia, hypocrisy, subjugation of women, and the treatment of homosexuals. However, serving the church has also allowed me to serve many other people. Many people have been able to beat addictions, recover from tragedies, and find reasons to live based on the teachings of the church."

"I have no doubt of that, Betty," Jasper said. "However, I believe you're not giving yourself enough credit. I've only known you for a day, but I can tell you're a very giving person. I think having a wonderful, caring person like you, or a group of caring people, helped these individuals more than the church."

"Thank you," Betty said as she bowed her head slightly. "But all I do is follow the teachings of Jesus, who teaches us to be kind, loving, and humble."

"If all Christians followed all the teachings of Christ that would be great," Jasper replied. "Unfortunately, many Christian churches and parishes have strayed from Jesus's teachings and now teach fear, hate, greed, and intolerance."

"That's true," Betty said. "You don't sound like a practicing Catholic."

"I'm sorry, but Ingrid here misled you a bit. Her heart was in the right place, but I'm a lapsed Catholic. I'm culturally a Catholic and went to church with my mom and dad when I lived with them. But after they passed away, I stopped going to church."

"So, what are you?" Betty asked.

"I guess I'm a Seeker," Jasper replied. "I want to leave my beliefs open to new information and experiences. Catholics may be right, Jews may be right, Buddhists may be right, or atheists may be right. I don't know, and I don't believe anyone else really knows either."

Suddenly Ingrid interjected, "I'm sorry I misled you Betty. We really wanted to see the documents you had, and I let myself fall into a lie. Please forgive me."

"That's okay," Betty replied. "I could tell pretty early on that you were looking for something specific and not merely information on your ancestor. Could you tell me what you were looking for?"

Jasper and Ingrid told Betty the truth and the entire story about Riley, his likely kidnapping, Emerson's story, the painting, and that they thought Emerson brought the object to Moriah to be looked at by one of the local miners.

Betty listened intently and paused in her own thoughts after Jasper and Ingrid had finished.

"I see," Betty finally said. "Well, you're welcome to continue looking through what we have in the museum, but I don't think it will help you."

"I don't think so either," Jasper replied.

"So, did your ancestor live in the area during the time you believe Emerson arrived with the object and the former slave?"

"Yes," Jasper replied. "My great, great, great granduncle was Father Clarence Brennan. He served as a priest in the area in the mid-1800s."

"How do you know this?" Betty asked.

"My father told me. Even though he was a relative on my mother's side, my father was really into genealogy and did some research on my mother's side of the family."

"Do you have any of your father's research materials on this Father Brennan?"

"Maybe," Jasper replied. "Why do you ask?"

"Well, I have a theory on what may have happened to Emerson, his black companion, and the object you've been looking for. Would you like to hear it?"

"Absolutely!" Jasper said.

"The mining community was a really rough place during the mid-1800s," Betty said. "There were lots of men looking for quick riches, not many women, and a very weak government and police force funded by the mining company. Many crimes were never reported or discovered, especially assaults and stealing."

"Okay," Jasper said. "So, what do you think happened?"

"Well, I think that there's a very good chance that Emerson and his black friend were robbed and the object you're seeking could have been stolen or lost during the attack. A well-dressed city boy from Boston and an African-American would have looked out of place and been easy targets. In addition, the authorities wouldn't have been any help to these outsiders and it's likely nothing would have been reported or investigated. Emerson may have been so upset about the attack and the lack of support from his fellow Northerners, that he may have left it out of any of his journals or writings."

"That is quite a theory," Jasper said.

"It is," Ingrid agreed. "But it would explain why Emerson never mentioned the object again in his journals and no record of him or the object was in any of the newspapers."

"Okay, Betty," Jasper said. "Let's say that your theory is correct. If you were us, what would be your next step in trying to find information about this object?"

"That's why I asked if you had any historical archives about Father Brennan," Betty said. "Although no confession of this crime would have been made to the authorities, most people in the area at that time were practicing Catholics. They needed to rid themselves of their guilt and they knew that Father Brennan would not share their confessions with anyone per church rules. But many priests back then did keep journals of people's confessions. Father Brennan may have as well and may have a confession and some information on the object you're seeking."

"Jasper, where do you think your father's information on Father Brennan may be?" Ingrid interjected.

"I'm not sure," Jasper replied. "I went through my father's records after he died, and I only remember files about his side of the family. I gave many of his documents to The Stone Society per his wishes."

"That's too bad," Betty said.

"But," Jasper added. "There is quite a bit of my dad's genealogical material at my family's lake house on Chazy Lake. If there's any information on Father Brennan, that's where it would be."

They finished their meal and Ingrid and Jasper both gave Betty a hug goodbye. Betty wished them luck as they all walked out of the restaurant.

As Jasper and Ingrid got to the car, Jasper said, "I think I'll stay at Chazy Lake tonight. I can start looking through my dad's genealogical research material first thing in the morning. However, I think the people who attacked us at the ski jumps probably know about my family's lake house. So, I think it would be safer for you to spend the night somewhere else."

"But what about you? You won't be safe there."

"I'll have to take that chance," Jasper replied. "It's the only place that could have the information we need to help find Riley and find the artifact. But I don't want to put you in harm's way. Is there a friend in Elizabethtown you could stay with?"

"I guess so," Ingrid replied. "My friend Gina and her husband live outside of town next to the state police station."

Ingrid called Gina, who said she would be happy to have Ingrid stay however long she needed.

Half an hour later, Jasper stopped the car outside of Gina's place.

"I don't want to leave you," Ingrid said, wiping tears from her eyes.

"I don't want to leave you either. But I cannot let you take this chance. I love you too much to put you in any more danger."

Jasper shuddered as he realized he had just told Ingrid he loved her. But he did love her, so he might as well let her know.

A smile broke through Ingrid's tears and she said, "I love you too. And because I love you I will stay here tonight as you've asked. But I'll be at your lake house first thing in the morning to help you. Is that clear?"

"Yes ma'am."

Ingrid leaned over and kissed Jasper. Jasper had forgotten what it felt like to really be kissed by someone who loved him. It felt like Ingrid was giving him energy that he had been missing all his life.

As their lips parted Ingrid smiled and said, "Don't give up. We will find answers and Riley. See you tomorrow."

Chapter 17

"What you do speaks so loudly that I cannot hear what you say."

~ Ralph Waldo Emerson

Atlanta, GA – October 2035

"They got away."

Billy Oscar squirmed in his chair at Secretary Joel Robertson's office. He was recounting the events of the night in Lake Placid and had reached the point of the story when Ingrid and Jasper had slid down the 120-meter ski jump.

"What do you mean, they got away?" Joel asked.

Billy continued his story.

"By the time John and I struggled down the elevator and limped back to the parking lot at the site, Jasper and Ingrid had escaped in their car. John and I returned to the bottom of the ski jump, picked up Mark's body, dragged it into the trunk of my car, and left. John asked me if he could take his brother back to the Midwest Republic to be buried. I told John that was too dangerous and told him to turn down an unmarked dirt road outside of Lake Placid and we would bury him there.

"John turned down the dirt road and drove about a mile before he stopped the car and popped the trunk. John and I walked to the back of the car and took Mark's body out of the car and placed it on the ground. After we placed Mark on the ground I saw John pick up the tire iron out of the trunk. Just as I was about to ask him what he needed the tire iron for, John hit me in the side of the head and I went unconscious.

"By the time I woke up, it was the next morning. John, Mark, and the car were gone. I still had my wallet, so I walked into town, rented a car, and drove back here as soon as I could. Please forgive me. I will make this right."

"I think you've done enough," Joel said. He got up from his office chair and lit a cigarette. "I thought I told you to only follow them."

"You said to follow them only if it seemed like they were still making progress," Billy said. "The information we were getting out of Riley didn't match the places they were investigating. So, I thought they were expendable."

"Where is Riley?" Joel said.

"He's being watched by one of my men at my compound in Lynchburg, Virginia."

"I know where that is," Joel said. "I will send a few of my men down to get him."

"I want to make this right," Billy said. "Can you at least use me to stake out Serenity Village or Jasper's house?"

"Now that they have been spooked by your incompetence, they would be idiots to go back to either place. Do either of them have immediate family in the area?"

"Not really," Billy said. "All of Ingrid's family is in Chile and Jasper's brother and his family is in the Pacific Republic."

"They have no other places they could stay near Lake Placid?"

"Jasper does own a lake house with his brother at Chazy Lake that they rent out," Billy said. "Perhaps I could go there and check it out for you?"

"That's not necessary," Joel said. "Leave the address of the lake house with my secretary outside."

"I'm so sorry sir. Please forgive me," Billy fell to his knees in front of Joel's desk.

"Rise, my son," Joel said as he walked over to Billy and helped him up. "As Jesus forgives all our sins, I forgive you. Please go in peace."

"Thank you," Billy said as he walked out of the office.

Joel walked over to the window and took another drag of his cigarette. He picked up his private phone and texted another contractor he used from time to time.

Are you available for a job?

- I am

Billy Oscar. I will send you a picture. 25 Lamp Way, Lynchburg, Virginia. Same price as always. Take care of him.

- Got it.

Chapter 18

"Make your own Bible. Select and collect all the words and sentences that in all your readings have been to you like the blast of a trumpet."

~ Ralph Waldo Emerson

Chazy Lake, NY – October 2035

Jasper's parents had left the lake house to Jasper and his brother. Although they each spent some time there, they also used it to make a little extra money. Rich families from New York City and New Jersey who had weathered the Great Secession of 2030 still wanted to take summer vacations in the Adirondacks. The highspeed train from New York City to Plattsburgh made that even easier, so Jasper and his brother were getting pretty good weekly rental rates for the lake house.

As it was late fall, there were no renters and the place was empty. As Jasper drove through Plattsburgh, he became depressed by how the city closest to the lake house had changed for the worse. Before the secession it had been a nice, quiet college town with a mix of retirees, professors, students, and some rough-around-the-edges locals, but all basically decent people. Now the border town was filled with smugglers, drug dealers, and prostitutes. Although there were still some decent local people and the university was still there, it seemed every year things got worse.

Being a border town to Canada used to be an asset, but now it was a detriment. Thousands of migrants from the southern republics, Mexico, and Central America streamed up to the border towns every year trying to cross into Canada. Not many got through the well protected Canadian border, so most of them ended up in cities right across the border. The northern republics tried to help, but they did not have the money or resources to really solve the situation.

Canada constantly struggled to stem the tide of illegal aliens from the republics. When the US broke up into six separate republics after the Great Secession of 2030, many of the republics hoped to be annexed by Canada.

Canada refused, but negotiated a deal that allowed an influx of one million legal immigrants from each republic each year and food subsidies in exchange for military protection. This agreement led to the North America Alliance that merged the US Armed Forces with the Canadian Armed Forces. This arrangement worked well for Canada and the six republics, as a large military was required to balance power against the Asian Allied Forces and the Russian Force.

Although the US republics and Canada shared armed forces, their governments could not be more different. Canada led the world in agricultural production and overall economic growth. Jasper remembered his father talking about Canada as a friendly and unassuming neighbor. He would wistfully remember Canada as a utopia with friendly people, untouched wilderness, and a generous welfare state with free health care for all.

Canada was nothing like a utopia in the year 2035. To feed its growing population and continue to grow the economy, Canada removed most environmental protections and used almost all its land for housing, commercial development, farming, or mining. Canada had "evolved" from a beautiful democratic socialist state to a hyper-capitalistic society like China or US in the early 2000s. While major land owners and corporate executives in Canada made obscene amounts of money, most Canadians eked out a living doing service and robotic repair jobs.

Leaving Plattsburgh, Jasper picked up some groceries and supplies in Dannemora. Made briefly famous during the Prison Break of 2015, Dannemora was still the sleepy small-town Jasper remembered when he was growing up. It had a few restaurants and stores but was dominated by the thirty-foot cement prison wall on the north side of Main Street.

Most of the residents of Dannemora were employed at the federal prison. They worked as guards, administrative workers, or as computer scientists who programmed and maintained the virtual reality rehabilitation machines.

Virtual reality was everywhere, and the republic governments were not afraid to use it for their own means. Due to the continued callousness and greed of their populations, every republic was more or less a police state, even the more liberal Northeast Republic. The death penalty had been eliminated due to the high cost of appeals, and empathy VR therapy was the new treatment used in the penal system across the US republics. The prison in Dannemora was the empathy VR therapy center for the Northeast Republic. The therapy consisted of using virtual reality on criminals to attempt to make them feel what their victims felt.

So, if you were a rapist, you spent two hours every day on a virtual reality simulation getting raped in the worst ways possible. The empathy VR therapy worked, but it worked too well.

Most criminals could not survive the treatment. They either went crazy or found unique ways to kill themselves. Prisons no longer tried to stop criminals from killing themselves. It was expensive to hold prisoners, and there was too little food for too many people anyway.

It was difficult to get computer programmers and technicians to work in the Dannemora prison. At first, they tried to bring in computer programmers from the city, but none of them lasted more than six months in the boring and uncultured North Country. In a move of desperation, the prison set up free local training programs for computer programming and promised twice the pay of a typical prison guard salary. Not many older locals took the training, but younger locals recently out of high school had grown up with computers and saw a great path to a well-paying job.

Finally, Jasper reached the lake house about ten minutes after leaving Dannemora. It was quiet around the lake this time of year, with no boats on the lake and few cars on the road. Many of the residences on the lake were only summer places, so many houses were empty a good portion of the year. In the dark and cold Jasper found the hidden key in the shed and opened the house. It smelled a bit musty but was clean and well cared for. Jasper's cousins lived next door and they took care of the cleaning and managed the rentals. It was easy extra income for them, and they could screen the potential renters to avoid any troublemakers.

After packing away the groceries, the clothes, and his personal items Jasper cooked a quick meal and went straight to bed.

~ ~ ~

Jasper was jolted awake by a dream. The sheets were soaked with sweat and his heart was pounding. As he started reliving that dream in his head, Jasper heard the downstairs door creak open. Shit, Jasper thought to himself. He must have forgotten to lock it...

Of course, they know about the lake house, Jasper thought. He was hoping they might not be able to find out because it was in his brother's name, but that was a naive thing to believe. Jasper knew there were some guns in the house, but he had no idea where they were or where the ammunition was. His father had a large collection of guns but had been very unorganized in storing them.

Jasper was without any weapon to defend himself. He could call 911, but by the time they came it would not make a difference. Jasper looked around the room looking for some kind of weapon. The only thing he could find was a hockey stick that his brother, Matt, had put up on the wall. It was signed by Austin Matthews, arguably the best Toronto Maple Leaf's hockey player in history. He had won five Stanley Cups, three MVP Awards, and to top it all off, he was an American. The best American hockey player ever by a long shot. He was Matt's favorite hockey player, and maybe his favorite person in the world that he was not married to or related to. He had gotten his autograph while playing at an outdoor pickup hockey game in Lake Placid.

Jasper whispered an apology to his brother as he took the stick off the wall. As he started walking downstairs Jasper heard someone clanging around in the living room. It only sounded like one person. They were not being loud, but they were not trying to be quiet either. Jasper decided his only asset was the element of surprise, so he slowly walked down the stairs as quietly as possible. When he reached the bottom of the stairs, Jasper sprinted into the living room, screaming like a banshee and wielding the hockey stick over his head.

"Jesus Christ!" said Ingrid as she dropped her backpack. "You scared the shit out of me."

"I scared the shit out of you?" Jasper said. "I was about to whack you on the side of the head with a hockey stick. What are you doing here?"

"I couldn't let you sleep alone in this house tonight, so I borrowed Gina's car and drove here. I missed you and wanted to be with you tonight no matter what the consequences might be."

"You did not seem to miss me too much at your retreat or after our experience at the ski jump," Jasper replied.

"Well, I had to be careful. The Brahma Kumaris strive for detachment and celibacy."

"And what do followers of Emerson Transcendentalists strive for?"

"In the words of Ralph Waldo Emerson, 'Leave all for love'." Ingrid kissed Jasper and they both fell to the floor.

Chapter 19

"Write it on your heart that every day is the best day in the year."

~ Ralph Waldo Emerson

Jasper woke up feeling better than he had in years. He was still very worried about Riley but having Ingrid back in his life brought a strength and purpose back to him. Jasper watched Ingrid sleep for a while before he got up and started to make breakfast. While stirring the pancake batter, Jasper started thinking about where his dad might have left information about Father Brennan.

Jasper's father was a packrat and probably would have become a full-blown hoarder if not for the moderating influence of his mother. When Jasper's dad passed away, it took Jasper and his brother almost a full week to go through all the stuff that he had hoarded at the lake house. This included random pieces of metal and wood stashed in the shed for future projects never started, piles of old magazines, including years and years of National Geographic, scuba diving magazines, windsurfing magazines, tropical fish magazines, old computers, scanners, old printers, and finally, all the genealogical research that he had compiled.

Jasper and his brother threw away about ninety percent of their father's stuff during "The Purge" as they called it, but they kept all his genealogy research because Jasper and his brother knew how important it had been to him.

"Wow, you're making pancakes?" Ingrid said as she walked into the kitchen.

"I am," Jasper replied. "And I have real maple syrup."

"Where did you get real maple syrup? I thought all the maple trees in the US went extinct."

"They did," Jasper said. "But you can get maple syrup from Canada in Plattsburgh. Cost me fifty dollars for a pint but I really wanted some."

As they ate the pancakes and carefully allocated the maple syrup, Ingrid asked, "So, do you know where your father's info on Father Brennan might be?"

"Well, I don't know if he actually has any or not, but if it's anywhere it would be above the garage. That's where my brother and I left all my father's genealogy research after he passed away."

"Is it organized in any way?" Ingrid asked.

"You met my dad," Jasper replied. "What do you think?"

Ingrid laughed. "I would guess not. But didn't you and your brother organize it?"

"No," Jasper replied. "We kept it all, but it would have taken us another week to organize it. Let me take a shower and then we'll go up there and start looking through it."

About twenty minutes later Jasper and Ingrid walked from the lake house to the garage. They both put on fleece jackets as there was no heat above the garage and it was about fifty degrees and windy. The area above the garage had originally been built as an extra bedroom for grandkids when Jasper's parents were living at the lake house. However, Jasper's father soon filled it up with junk, and his parents only got one grandkid from Jasper's brother, so it never became the bedroom it was meant to be. Now it was storage for family stuff, and Jasper and his brother kept it locked up and separate from the lake house rental.

Jasper unlocked the door in the back of the garage and they climbed a flight of wooden stairs to the attic. It was a typical pitched roof attic over a two-car garage; you could stand up in the middle of the room, but you had to crouch down to get to the sides of the attic. The genealogy research was piled on both sides of the room in random binders, folder, books, and loose papers.

"Didn't your father store any of his research digitally?" Ingrid asked.

"He did," Jasper said. "But most of his computer files were about his side of the family, and a lot of it was on old flash drives that were damaged. The rest was saved on older computers that I don't think work anymore. I think our best chance of finding anything on my mother's side of the family is to go through whatever he may have had in the printed records."

"So how about we start from the back of the room," Ingrid said. "You take the right side and I'll take the left side."

"Sounds like a plan," Jasper replied.

Jasper and Ingrid started into their respective piles. It went quickly as they were only looking for anything related to Brennan or the Port Henry and Moriah areas. Much of the research was related to the Stone family and their background, which they could set aside. The archives and research consisted of headstone pictures, old census lists, voter rolls, newspaper clippings, diaries, and journals.

About an hour into the search Jasper pulled away a pile of Stone Society newsletters to reveal a box labeled "Brennan."

"Ingrid, look here."

As Ingrid walked over, Jasper pulled the box toward the center of the room. The box was an old microwave box filled with papers, binders, and books.

"Awesome," Ingrid said as she pulled out a few binders.

"Glad we at least found something," Jasper said. He pulled out a few books and papers from the top of the box.

The first thing they examined was a mixture of old newspaper articles, mostly about the Dannemora area. Jasper's grandfather was born in Dannemora and there were articles circled about his years of service with the military police and the Dannemora Prison. The most interesting article was about Eleanor Roosevelt visiting Dannemora while FDR was the governor of New York. Mrs. Roosevelt had visited Jasper's great-grandfather's house in Dannemora because he and his wife had been heavily involved in local Democratic Party politics. The documents included photographs of Jasper's great grandparents with Mrs. Roosevelt in their old house.

Interesting stuff, Jasper thought, but not what he was looking for. Jasper and Ingrid got through the remaining newspaper articles on top of the box and came upon an old tattered journal with faded yellow pages and no label on the plain black cover. Jasper opened the book delicately and read the inside cover: "Diary of Father John Brennan 1850-1870."

"Holy shit."

"What is it?" Ingrid asked.

"I think I found Father Brennan's diary," Jasper said.

"Let me see," Ingrid said as she sat down beside Jasper.

Jasper slowly opened the journal and placed it on the floor. He then placed a book over each side of the journal to keep the pages open.

"Alright," Jasper said. "Let's go through it together."

The journal was hard to read because Father Brennan wrote in cursive, which was rarely used or taught in school anymore, but Jasper and Ingrid were able to fumble their way through it. They read through each page silently together, and Jasper slowly turned the pages after confirming that Ingrid had finished reading.

It was boring reading. It was mostly records of local baptisms, weddings, and funerals. These were broken up by brief descriptions of visits to the local church in Moriah by family, friends, the bishop, and other local priests. Sometimes Father Brennan would go to other towns in northern New York or Vermont to help another parish or take a few days to himself. These descriptions were dull as well and were limited to his observations of the parish, the meals, and the other priests.

To his credit, Father Brennan seemed to have been a good, decent, and kind man. If he thought ill of anyone, he never wrote it down in his journal. All he had were kind words for his parishioners, his family, his fellow priests, and the beauty of the Adirondacks. He spent his free time fishing and walking around the local woods and lakes. He occasionally would enjoy an ale or a whisky but seemed to never overconsume.

He seemed to be a textbook pious and simple Irish Catholic priest. But that did not help Jasper any.

Father Brennan only had one entry per day, which he would do in the evening right after he had eaten supper.

But one day, he had an additional entry first thing in the morning:

September 23, 1860

I did not sleep well at all. A terrible thing happened in the night I cannot explain, and it has shaken me and my faith. It began with Mary banging on my door early this morning. She was sick with despair and worry as she had found a mysterious object that seemed to be filled with evil spirits…

Chapter 20

"It is easy to live for others, everybody does.
I call on you to live for yourself."

~ Ralph Waldo Emerson

Moriah, NY – September 1860

Jacob Spellman wiped the sweat off his brow and heaved the last load of rocks from the rail car to the waste pile. He had finished his twelve-hour shift and was ready to walk home to see his wife, Mary, and his two sons. He knew he should stay for the Catholic service conducted by Father Brennan after every shift, but he did not feel like it today. He knew Father Brennan would tell Mary that he missed Jacob at the service, but Jacob was bone tired and that was a worry for another day. It was a late afternoon in September, so Jacob decided to take the scenic route back to the house along the creek. While the other men headed to the local bar to throw a few back, Jacob liked to use the few moments of freedom to clear his mind and enjoy the beauty of the mountains and streams surrounding the dirty iron ore mine and its even dirtier workers.

As Jacob strolled along the trail next to the creek, he noticed something on the edge of the creek reflecting the late afternoon sunlight. Probably a pickaxe or a piece of rusty metal, Jacob thought as he carefully walked down to the edge of the creek. Everything in town was owned by the mining company, so he would have to return whatever he found to the company. If he tried to keep anything, the local police, who were the stooges of the mine owners, would quickly turn him in and he would have his pay garnished or he would be fired. This thought made Jacob hesitate for a second. Why should he haul whatever this thing was out of the creek when he would just have to lug it back to work tomorrow?

But his curiosity got the better of him and he bushwhacked his way to the edge of the creek. When he got to the object, he could tell immediately that it was no tool of the mine. It was made of some kind of rock, but not any rock Jacob had ever come across. It was rectangular and about three feet wide by two feet long. Jacob realized it was completely white in color as he wiped away the mud caked onto it. Once enough mud was cleared from the edges, Jacob grasped ahold of it and prepared himself for a difficult lift with a piece of rock this large. Instead, Jacob ended up falling on his ass as he pulled it out of the mud. The object was extremely light in weight, at most five pounds. As Jacob wiped off the remaining mud and examined it, he realized it looked even stranger than he originally thought. One whole side consisted of something that felt and looked like a mirror but was not reflecting anything.

Jacob had no idea what this object was but was sure it did not belong to the mine. Jacob had worked there for four years after arriving from Ireland and had used about every machine or tool the company owned. He had never seen anything like this, and he sure as hell was not going to give it to the greedy rich mine owners.

Finally breaking out from his obsession with the object, Jacob looked up to make sure he was not being watched or that anyone had seen him. Feeling confident that no one had seen him, Jacob slowly trudged back up to the trail. The shift change was over by this time, so Jacob felt if he was careful, he could sneak the object into his family's shack without anyone seeing him.

Jacob kept to the woods as much as possible on his walk home. Although some leaves had started falling from the trees, there was still enough cover to keep him hidden. Finally, reaching the back of his shack, he sprinted past the community outhouse, across the open field, and into the back door of his shack.

"Jacob! You scared the devil out of me," his wife Mary cried as she grasped onto her shirt. "What in God's name is that?"

"I have no idea. It's like nothing I've ever seen before."

"Well, put it away before the kids see it. I don't want them getting any ideas."

"Okay," Jacob replied meekly. "Aren't you curious what it is?"

"No, I am not. Curiosity is the work of the devil," Mary replied. "Remember that teacher who put those crazy ideas into Peter and Thomas's heads before she was fired? Talking to them all about science and strange theories that we may have been begat by other animals. The children pestered us for weeks about if there really was a God and if Adam and Eve were real. It took months of prayer and church to get those ideas out of their minds. So, put it away."

Jacob nodded in compliance and put the object under the extra blankets that they used during the cold winter months. As he finished hiding the object, Peter and Thomas came in the door of the shack after playing outside with their friends.

"Dinner is ready," Mary told the children. "Sit down and your father will say grace."

Dinner went forward as it always did. Jacob said grace and Peter and Thomas talked about school and their friends while Jacob listened intently. Mary listened as well, but only for the opportunity to chide the boys for their use of language or to tell them she didn't approve of them playing with the Protestant children in the camp.

After dinner, the boys and Jacob helped with cleanup and sat down for the daily Bible reading. Mary could not read, so it was on Jacob to pick the scripture. Jacob chose the Book of Ecclesiastes from the Old Testament.

Jacob partially chose this book to make Mary upset. He was mad he could not share the object he found with his sons and he knew that Mary did not enjoy this book of the Bible. The book came from a king, who relayed his experiences and drew lessons from them. He discussed the meaning of life and the best way to live. He proclaimed all actions of man to be inherently futile, as both wise and foolish actions end in death.

Wanting to keep the readings short so he could investigate the object, Jacob read only three passages from Ecclesiastes. He spoke slowly to try to understand the texts himself and make sure the boys could follow the meanings as well.

First, he read Ecclesiastes 1:13-17:

"And I applied my heart to seek and to search out by wisdom all that is done under heaven. It is an unhappy business that God has given to the children of man to be busy with. I have seen everything that is done under the sun, and behold, all is vanity and a striving after wind. What is crooked cannot be made straight, and what is lacking cannot be counted. I said in my heart, 'I have acquired great wisdom, surpassing all who were over Jerusalem before me, and my heart has had great experience of wisdom and knowledge.' And I applied my heart to know wisdom and to know madness and folly. I perceived that this also is but a striving after wind."

Then he moved onto Ecclesiastes 8:17:

"Then I saw all the work of God, that man cannot find out the work that is done under the sun. However, much man may toil in seeking, he will not find it out. Even though a wise man claims to know, he cannot find it out."

Finally, he read Ecclesiastes 3:18-20:

"I said in my heart with regard to the children of man that God is testing them that they may see that they themselves are but beasts. For what happens to the children of man and what happens to the beasts is the same; as one dies, so dies the other. They all have the same breath, and man has no advantage over the beasts, for all is vanity. All go to one place. All are from the dust, and to dust all return."

"What do you think these passages mean?" Jacob asked the boys.

Jacob always asked the boys what they thought the passages meant. Another thing Mary hated. Mary thought only Father Brennan should tell the boys what the Bible was trying to say.

"That we don't have to go school!" Peter said, making Thomas laugh.

"Peter, stop it!" Mary yelled. A quick smile formed on Jacob's lips and quickly disappeared.

"No, it does not mean that," Jacob stated. "Thomas, what do you think these passages mean?"

"That there are some things about God that we will never know," Thomas replied.

"Very good," said Jacob. "There are things about God and the world that we will never know. But we should always try to understand the world and God better each day. Even though there are some things we will never understand, striving to figure them out is its own reward. And in the process, we might discover some interesting things about ourselves."

"Time for bed, children," Mary interjected.

As the children started to climb into bed in the back room, Mary gave Jacob a disappointing look.

"What did I do?" Jacob asked.

"What you always do," Mary replied. "You confuse the boys with your interpretation of the Bible. Leave that to Father Brennan. I'm going to bed. Please do not stay up too late. Goodnight."

"Goodnight, Mary," Jacob replied.

Jacob sat down in his favorite chair and lit his pipe. This was his favorite part of the day. A few minutes to relax, enjoy the taste of the tobacco, and reflect.

The rest of his day consisted of work, eating, children, wife, sleep, and then doing the whole thing over again. Jacob felt gratitude for what he had, but he always felt something was missing. Most people in the town felt comforted by the teachings of the church. Jacob, however, did not. Jacob believed in God, but felt the church was run the wrong way. He had read the Bible, just as Father Brennan had, but had a much different interpretation of it. Why should priests be the only ones to interpret the Bible passages? And how do we know the Bible is the Word of God? Maybe it is only stories to help you through your life. Maybe Jesus was only a teacher and not a God?

Jacob tried talking to Mary about things like this, but she wanted no part of it. Meanwhile, the children were too young, and Jacob did not want to confuse them at this point in their lives. His friends were good people but simple. Their only concerns were work, gambling, church, and their families. If he talked about his thoughts and doubts with Father Brennan, he knew Father Brennan would only quote Bible sayings and report his "evil thoughts" to his wife.

So, Jacob had no one to talk to about his thoughts and he could only sit in the quiet and try to grasp at something he could not quite reach. But tonight, he could examine the strange object he found. He threw aside the blankets covering it and placed the object in his lap. The whole thing was white and smooth. Light in his hands, he closely examined each side of the object. As he was holding it, suddenly a sound emanated from it. It sounded like the organ in church except cleaner and much quieter.

A light pulsed out from the object. Jacob turned it over and stared into the light.

CHAPTER 21

"Let us be silent, that we may hear the whisper of God."

~ Ralph Waldo Emerson

MORIAH, NY – SEPTEMBER 1860

Mary's eyes popped open as she jumped out of bed. Drenched in sweat and breathing rapidly, Mary slowly became aware of where she was. She was thankful she did not wake the two boys, who were still asleep in the other bed. Mary finally slowed her breathing when she realized it was only a nightmare and she was safe in her family's small cabin in northern New York.

Turning to her right, she was surprised to find the other side of the bed empty. It was very early in the morning, and she usually awoke before Jacob to start breakfast. She got up and quietly walked toward the kitchen.

As she walked into kitchen, she shrieked in shock. Her husband was lying on the floor with his arms out and his eyes wide open. Mary rushed over and sat by Jacob's side.

"Jacob, wake up!" she pleaded as she shook Jacob's lifeless body. Jacob did not wake up and Mary quietly wept at his side.

Although they were not deeply in love, Jacob was a good man and a good provider who never raised a hand to her. He worked hard at the iron ore mine, was a doting father to their two sons, and dutifully went to church every Sunday. Mary felt lucky to be his wife, but now he was gone.

"Jacob? What happened to you?" Mary spoke aloud between bouts of weeping. There were no signs of struggle and the door was still locked from the inside. Mary had heard of some older men dying in this way, but never someone as young as Jacob.

After a few more minutes of crying, Mary pulled herself together and knelt next to Jacob's corpse and prayed. She prayed for Jacob's soul to reach God and heaven. She prayed for her two fatherless boys and she prayed for the strength to carry on with her life.

As she stumbled to her feet, Mary caught sight of the old rocking chair Jacob loved so much. Underneath the rocking chair was the strange object that Jacob had found last night. The object was the shape of a rock but made of a material Mary had never seen before. It was white with smooth corners and a smooth finish. One side had a light emanating from it.

Mary jumped over to the chair and turned over the object so she could not see what the other side was showing. She knew that object was the devil's making when Jacob brought it home last night, and now she was sure it was the cause of Jacob's death.

Mary was scared and confused. Anytime she was scared or confused in the past, she asked Father Brennan for help. He always told her what to do and what to think of the unknowns that tormented her. She knew she must see Father Brennan now and ask him what to do with this evil object.

Mary wanted to leave right away, but she did not want the children to see Jacob like he was. Mary took Jacob by the collar, dragged his body back into bedroom, and struggled to pull his lifeless body back on the bed. She found the strength to get Jacob on the bed and cover him from head to toe with blankets. Hopefully, when the children woke up, they would think their father was still sleeping in bed and would not investigate further.

Mary went back to the kitchen. She hurriedly put on her shoes, threw on her coat, and grabbed the object, making sure she did not look at the light. It was dawn as she opened the door to the cabin. There was nobody outside the mining compound cabins and she could not see any candlelight in any windows.

Hunched over to conceal the object, Mary headed straight to Father Brennan's small cabin next to the town church. It was only a five-minute walk away, but it seemed like an eternity to Mary. She wanted answers and to get rid of this evil in her hands.

Finally, she reached the priest's cabin and banged on the door. "Father Brennan, it's Mary Spellman. Please open up, something terrible has happened."

Mary heard footsteps inside and the wooden door quickly swung open. Father Brennan was dressed in a tattered long undergarment and wore thick stockings on his feet. Mary had never seen him in anything but his priestly robes and would normally be embarrassed to see him this way, but then all she wanted was answers.

"Mary, what's wrong?" Father Brennan slurred, rubbing his eyes.

"Jacob is dead," Mary blurted out between the tears that had arisen again. "I don't know what to do."

"There, there, my dear," said Father Brennan as Mary fell into his arms. "It will be alright. Let me put on some clothes and we can go to him together."

As Father Brennan put on his robes and his boots he noticed the object in Mary's hands. "What are you holding my child?"

Mary told Father Brennan of the object Jacob had found the day before and that she had found it next to him the following morning.

"Let me see it." Father Brennan reached his hand toward Mary.

Mary handed the object to Father Brennan. The light from the object had disappeared and the priest closely analyzed it.

"There is evil in this object," Father Brennan said. "We must get rid of it and you must not tell anyone about it. Do you understand?"

"Yes," Mary replied. "But what is it and why did it kill Jacob?"

"I believe this object was made by the devil and it poisoned Jacob's mind. We must hide it where no one can ever find it."

"But where?" asked Mary.

Father Brennan fell deep in thought. Where could this thing be hidden where it could not be found again?

"The lake!" Father Brennan finally blurted out.

"What?"

"Mary, this object must be hidden at the bottom of the lake. Your father has a canoe at the lake, is that correct?"

"Yes Father, he uses it for fishing."

"I will go to the house to pray for Jacob's soul and explain what happened to the children. You must get rid of this devilish thing in the middle of the lake."

"I don't know if I can, Father," Mary said.

"Please Mary. Leave now before it gets too light and people see you. I will meet you at the house when you return. I know this is difficult, but you will have God's strength within you to help you with this task."

"Yes, Father," Mary replied as she took the object from Father Brennan's hand. Mary hunched over to hide the object and stepped out into the early morning dawn. A mist rose from open fields as Mary walked from the cabin to the lake road. Mary knew she must complete this important task for Father Brennan and The Lord. She straightened up and began her journey.

After about an hour of walking on the road, Mary reached the edge of the lake. Tired, but relieved she had not seen anyone, Mary headed toward her father's canoe, which was stashed on the edge of the lake. The early fall morning was beautiful as the sun peaked over the mountain on the eastern side of the lake and reflected sunlight on the lake mist.

Mary sighed with relief as she found the canoe where her father always left it. She carefully placed the object in the center of the canoe, took the paddle and pushed the canoe into the water. As the lake was calm, Mary made quick progress. Mary knew she needed to get far enough out in deeper water to guarantee the object would not be found.

After about fifteen minutes of steady paddling, Mary put the paddle inside the boat. Holding onto the object, she looked up to the sky and prayed, "Lord, please let the water of the lake mask the evil that this tool of the devil holds and never let it be found again."

Mary dropped the object into the cold lake water and slowly paddled the canoe back to shore.

Chapter 22

"Without ambition one starts nothing. Without work one finishes nothing. The prize will not be sent to you. You have to win it."

~ Ralph Waldo Emerson

Chazy Lake, NY – October 2035

September 23, 1860

I did not sleep well at all. A terrible thing happened last night that I cannot explain, and it has shaken me and my faith. It all started with Mary banging on my door early this morning. She was sick with despair and worry as she had found a mysterious object that seemed to be filled with evil spirits.

Mary believed that the object had killed her husband Jacob the night before after she retired to bed. As I examined the object and listened to Mary's story, I knew this evil object needed to be disposed of, so it could not harm anyone else. It was like nothing I had ever seen before. It was bright white and light as a feather even though I was sure it was made of some type of rock. After some thought, I told Mary to use her father's canoe to drop the object in the middle of the lake. I hoped this was the right thing to do.

"I know where it is!" Jasper yelled.

"How do you know what lake?" Ingrid asked.

"It has to be Lake Champlain," Jasper said. "It's the only large lake near Moriah."

"Okay," Ingrid replied. "But that's a pretty large goddamn lake. How do we know where she dumped it?"

"Let's look at a map," Jasper said as he opened his laptop.

Zooming in on a map of Moriah, Jasper pointed at the screen.

"The shortest distance from Moriah to Lake Champlain follows a current road directly to Port Henry," Jasper said. "That road most likely existed as a road or trail during the mid-1800s, so it's likely the way Mary took to get to her father's canoe."

Jasper was getting really excited and continued, "Because she had just walked about three miles carrying the object, I would guess she was pretty tired and didn't paddle that far out from Port Henry before she dumped the object in the water. Lake Champlain is narrow in that area, and sandy. It shouldn't be too difficult to find a white object by diving in that area as long as the visibility is pretty good."

Ingrid still looked doubtful. "How are we sure she dumped it in the lake? She could have kept it or lost it."

"She dumped it the lake because that's what Father Brennan told her to do," Jasper replied. "I know we don't do what priests tell us to do nowadays, but back then you did what the priest told you to do because you were sure you would go to hell if you didn't."

"Okay," Ingrid said. She looked a bit less doubtful but still not as optimistic as Jasper. "Do you still scuba dive? I thought you stopped diving after the incident in Florida during our last vacation together."

"No, I haven't been diving since that experience," Jasper said. The craziness of that incident flooded back into his consciousness.

~ ~ ~

Jasper was scuba diving with Ingrid in Florida when they ran into a huge manta ray that was six feet across and over ten feet long. They surprised it, and when it saw them it turned sharply and quickly swam away. As it turned, it knocked off a shark sucker that had been attached to its underside. Shark suckers, now extinct along with most sharks, were ugly scavenger fish that attached themselves to larger animals. The top of their heads contained suckers that would attach to the bottom of a ray or shark, and they would eat any small pieces of prey that would fall out of the larger fish's mouth as it was feeding.

Once that shark sucker fell off the manta ray, it went looking for a new large animal to attach itself to and decided that animal would be Jasper. As the ugly fish started swimming toward Jasper, he tried in vain to swim away and push it away, but it was much too fast for him to be successful in his efforts. After a short struggle, it decided to attach itself to the thigh of Jasper's short wetsuit. Jasper could have tried to pull the fish off, but that location was likely the most comfortable position he could have hoped for. It was not directly attached to his body, and Jasper could see the shark sucker without it being in his way.

Jasper could have returned to the boat, but they had just started their dive, and each had over forty-five minutes of air left. Ingrid signed to Jasper to ask if he wanted to return to the boat. Jasper shook his head 'No' and signed to her that he wanted to continue the dive. She gave the OK sign and Jasper attempted to continue the dive without thinking of the shark sucker that was attached to his wetsuit. As Jasper started kicking his fins to swim to the wreck they were diving near, Jasper saw a flash of silver out of the corner of his eye. The flash of silver then stopped in front of them and Jasper realized it was a large barracuda. Barracuda grew up to twelve feet long, had huge razor-sharp teeth, and were very territorial. While most fish would swim away as you approached them, even most sharks, barracudas would not move an inch and would stare you down as you swam by them. Lethal attacks were rare, but barracuda bites were not. They had terrible eyesight and would sometime mistake something shiny, like a diving knife or underwater camera, as a fish. A small but significant number of divers had been bitten and some of them had lost fingers or even entire hands.

As the barracuda stopped swimming, Jasper noticed that it had a fish in its mouth. As it thrashed its mouth back and forth, Jasper noticed that the fish looked like a shark sucker. Jasper looked down at his thigh where the shark sucker had been, and it was gone. Looking back at the barracuda, he realized that it had snatched the shark sucker off his thigh and was eating it.

After getting past the shock that the barracuda could have easily taken a chunk out of his thigh as it snatched the shark sucker, Jasper became elated. Not only had he rid himself of the shark sucker attached to his thigh, he was getting a front row seat to the barracuda catching and eating a meal. But the barracuda did not finish the job. For some reason, the barracuda released the shark sucker from its mouth. The shark sucker had a large chunk of flesh missing from its dorsal side and the surrounding water was filling with blood, but it had enough life left to start swimming away. As it tried to escape danger, it decided to return to the safety of the large animal it was previously attached to seconds ago. Jasper.

Jasper thought he had acted reasonably cool and calm up to this point, but he was ashamed to admit that he totally freaked out as this bleeding fish started swimming toward him. Jasper knew the danger of blood in the water, and he panicked as he imagined a feeding frenzy of barracuda and sharks wildly lunging at the bleeding shark sucker after it became attached to him again. As Jasper thrashed his arms and legs in a vain attempt to keep the wounded shark sucker from attaching to him again, Ingrid grasped Jasper and pulled him up to the surface.

When they reached the surface, Ingrid and Jasper pulled out their regulator mouthpieces.

"The shark sucker is attached to the back of your air tank and I can't get it off," Ingrid yelled as they bobbed up and down in waves. "Swim to the boat. I'll follow you and watch the barracuda."

Jasper didn't know what Ingrid would be able to do if the barracuda charged him and tried to snatch the bleeding shark sucker again, but he concentrated on locating the boat. Jasper scanned the horizon and located it about two hundred feet away. Having no desire to see what was going on below him, Jasper swam toward the boat as fast as he could.

Jasper finally reached the boat after a few minutes of swimming, and the captain noticed Jasper heading toward the back of the boat.

"Are you alright?" the captain asked. Jasper was back much earlier than anticipated. It had been about fifteen minutes since they all jumped off the boat to start the dive.

As Jasper clutched the rope and pulled himself toward the boat, he tried to tell the captain about the shark sucker and the barracuda. Jasper must have been difficult to understand because the captain gave him a confused look and reminded him to take off his fins before he started climbing the ladder on the back of the dive boat.

As the captain helped him onto the boat, he said, "Holy shit! You have a half-eaten shark sucker attached to the back of your air tank."

"I know," Jasper said breathlessly. The captain pulled the fish off Jasper's tank and threw it into the water.

~ ~ ~

"On a positive note," Jasper continued. "I became a minor celebrity at that dive company. Every year when I was back in that town, all the people working there remembered me and told me they shared that story anytime someone asked them the scariest or strangest thing that had happened on one of their dive trips."

"Do you think you can dive now?" Ingrid asked.

"I think I can," Jasper replied. "The only fish in Lake Champlain are catfish and carp. They're not dangerous."

"What about scuba equipment?" Ingrid asked.

"My dad was a serious scuba diver even into his eighties. He left me all his gear and it's here at the house. It should fit me."

"What about a boat?" Ingrid asked.

"Well, the boat here is in storage for the winter, but it would be pretty useless on Lake Champlain anyway."

"Why?" Ingrid asked.

"Lake Champlain has been decimated by invasive species, especially Eurasian milfoil. Eurasian milfoil has grown so out of control on the lake that it jams up any propeller motors. Almost everyone uses airboats on Lake Champlain nowadays."

"Why doesn't Chazy Lake have the same problem?" Ingrid asked.

"Chazy Lake has a dam, so they're able to lower the lake each year, which freezes and kills most of the milfoil. We used to have a problem with the milfoil here because too many people didn't want the lake lowered, thinking it would kill the fish. But it got so bad that they finally relented, and now everyone agrees it's the best way to keep the milfoil at bay. The fish swim to deeper water during the lowering on the lake, so they're fine."

"So where are we going to find an airboat?"

"My cousin Morgan lives outside Plattsburgh and has an airboat at Mooney Bay Marina," Jasper replied. "I'm sure he'll let us use it."

Jasper called Morgan and asked if he and Ingrid could use his airboat. Morgan said that was fine and that he would meet them at the marina the next morning.

Ingrid and Jasper spent the rest of the day digging out scuba gear and testing it to ensure it was still in good working condition. After a dinner of local corn on the cob and catfish, Jasper called Jennifer to see if there was any news on Riley. Jennifer said that the police agreed with their belief that Riley had likely been kidnapped. She said they told her they were following some leads but had nothing concrete yet. Jasper told Jennifer he'd had some success following Riley's information and would know more tomorrow.

After getting off the phone with Jennifer, Ingrid and Jasper shared a few beers and some stories about Riley before they went to bed.

Chapter 23

"A great man is always willing to be little."

~ Ralph Waldo Emerson

Lynchburg, VA – October 2035

"Hello, Riley Emerson Collins."

Riley told almost no one his middle name. Even Jasper didn't know it. So, when a tall, handsome, forty-something man who was dressed in an expensive navy suit said it as he opened the door to the interrogation room, Riley took notice.

A few minutes earlier, the only guard Riley had seen since the first day of his confinement told him to get out of the small cot in the interrogation room and sit in the chair. The guard told him a very important man was here to ask him some questions. This must be the man the guard was talking about.

Riley was still a bit woozy from his last injection. They gave him one injection a day of what he assumed was a type of "truth serum". The injections were not painful, but actually quite euphoric. About fifteen minutes after the injection, Riley fell into a semiconscious state. The best description Riley could come up to describe the effect of the drug was a mixture of how he felt when he got his wisdom teeth out and an intense acid trip he experienced in college. However, his memories of his time under the influence were very vague. He knew he must have given up some information, but he had really concentrated on at least not giving his interrogators all the details he knew. Riley really hoped he was not putting Jasper or Ingrid in danger.

"Who are you?" Riley said, trying to concentrate as best he could.

"My name is Joel Agassiz Robertson."

"Agassiz?' Riley said. "Are you a descendent of Dr. Louis Agassiz?"

"I am," Joel replied. "Just as you are a relative of Ralph Waldo Emerson."

"That's true," Riley said. "But at least my ancestor was a decent and kind man. Not a racist like Dr. Agassiz."

"Dr. Agassiz was not a racist," Joel said. "Louis Agassiz was a renowned biologist and geologist recognized as an innovative and prodigious scholar of Earth's natural history. He also made extensive contributions to animal classifications and to the study of geological history, including to the founding of glaciology. He is remembered as an amazing man who made vast institutional and scientific contributions to zoology and geology."

"That may be all he's known for down here in the Southern Republic," Riley said. "But in the rest of the world he's also known as a Darwinist denier and a major contributor to scientific racism."

"That's your opinion," Joel said. "Dr. Agassiz believed in a theory of human origin which posits the view that the human races are of different origins. That does not mean that one race is better or more evolved than another, they are just separate."

"Separate but equal," Riley said. "That sounds familiar. That was the 1950s southern doctrine for racial segregation. Which you're slowly trying to bring back now in the Southern Republic."

"That's not true," Joel said. "That's the fake news you're fed in the Northeast Republic. Polygenism is a scientific theory, like the theory of evolution or the theory of climate change."

"It's a theory that has been disproved," Riley said. "Modern research into our genes has proved that we all descend from the first humans in Africa. Agassiz's beliefs provided a scientific basis for slavery."

"Dr. Agassiz never supported slavery."

"That's the first true thing you've said," Riley stated. "But he did visit several plantations in 1850 while in South Carolina to address a meeting of scientists in Charleston on the topic of the 'separate creation' of the human races. That notion provided a scientific and natural basis for racial inequality and slavery. He must have been aware that what he was saying was an argument for slavery. And although he did not publicly support slavery, he was a racist. Shortly after he arrived in America, Agassiz encountered black servants in a Philadelphia hotel and, as he wrote to his mother, was completely unnerved by them. He wished he did not have to eat in front of them and was appalled to have any contact with them. Agassiz insisted in print that the descendants of Adam and Eve were decidedly Caucasian, that black men and women came from some other geographical region as a separate, distinct and inferior race, which should not be treated equally, and that the races should never mingle or marry."

"You know your history," Joel said. "Dr. Agassiz believed, as I believe, that the Book of Genesis recounts the origin of the white race only and that the animals and plants in the Bible refer only to those species proximate and familiar to Adam and Eve."

"Ah, now we get to the real point," Riley said. "Dr. Agassiz's theories help support your theology, which you've made the official religion of your republic. The truth is that Agassiz was so much on the wrong side of the debates about Darwin and race that when he died, he was almost totally isolated from the scientific community. He was stubborn, committed to bad science, and a media whore who claimed many other scientists' discoveries as his own."

"We each can believe what we want to believe. That is freedom."

"I agree," said Riley. "But you cannot use bad science to support your beliefs. Someday the people who follow you and your bastardization of Christianity will become enlightened and follow their own paths based on truth and decency. Then you won't have power over them anymore."

"Why do you hate Jesus?" Joel said.

"I don't hate Jesus," Riley replied. "His core teachings are about tolerance, humility, kindness, and love. Everyone should follow that, and if you followed his teachings the world would be a much better place. But the prosperity Christianity you proselytize has become a tribal religion based on fear and paranoia. You preach that people should fear Satan, or Muslims, or change, or new ways of thinking. This leads to an us vs. them mentality and eventually leads to violence."

Joel started getting upset. "The people need to be led, like the shepherd leads his flock. Most people aren't capable of determining truth for themselves. They get confused and troubled by change and new ideas. It's my job to keep them on the correct path. That's why I need to find this artifact you and your friends have been looking for. If it becomes public, my people will become confused and unsure about what is the truth."

"Bullshit!" said Riley. "It's only about control. People should question their beliefs. I question mine all the time.

No one knows what the truth of our existence is or if any religion is the 'true' religion. Could Christianity be the one 'true' religion? Sure, it could, but which sect? Catholicism, Greek Orthodox, Baptist, Methodists? But Atheism or Buddhism or Hinduism may also be true."

"Then why is a majority of advanced western civilizations Christian?"

"Most people follow the religion of their parents," Riley said. "The only reason the western world is Christian is because Emperor Constantine made Christianity the official religion of the Roman Empire. Then the Roman Empire conquered Europe and converted everyone to Christianity. Finally, the first settlers in America were from Europe, so the former United States became a Christian nation. If the Persian Empire had conquered Europe, you would be a follower of Islam."

"That's enough!" said Joel. "Your blasphemy will only make it easier to get rid of you when the time comes. And I think that time is rapidly approaching."

"What do you mean?" Riley said.

"We believe your friends are getting close to finding the artifact," Joel said. "I sent my own men to follow them and they think your friends made a huge breakthrough. I'm joining them up north tonight and I'm taking you with us. Once we have the artifact, you and your friends will be expendable."

Chapter 24

"Live in the sunshine, swim the sea, drink the wild air."

~ Ralph Waldo Emerson

Chazy Lake, NY – October 2035

The next morning, Jasper packed his scuba gear into the Trybrid and headed down to Mooney Bay with Ingrid. Mooney Bay Marina was located north of Plattsburgh on Point au Roche, a nice peninsula jutting out into Lake Champlain. Part of the peninsula was a New York State Park with nice hiking and biking trails. Money from rich Canadians supported the marina and the surrounding state park.

Because it was fall, Mooney Bay Marina was quiet when they pulled in and they quickly located Jasper's cousin Morgan. Morgan's tall and lean figure was leaning on the edge of the main office building as they arrived.

Morgan was maybe the kindest and politest person Jasper had ever met. Jasper had never seen him be anything but polite, helpful, patient, and kind. He was a world class triathlete but never boasted about it. If you asked him about it, he would answer any question you had, but would quickly change the subject and ask you something about your life. His mother, Mary, was an amazing woman who used to live next door to Jasper's parents. As Mary and Jasper's parents got older, Morgan and his sister Maureen would help them with any physical work that needed to be done. Jasper helped when he was there, but Morgan and Maureen were always helping whoever needed assistance in their family at any time.

"Morgan, it's good to see you," Jasper said, shaking his hand and giving him a quick bro-hug.

"It's good to see you, too," Morgan replied.

"This is Ingrid," Jasper said, pointing to Ingrid. "I think you met a long time ago."

"Yes," Morgan said as he shook Ingrid's hand. "It's nice to see you again."

"Hi Morgan, thank you so much for letting us use your boat."

"No problem," Morgan replied. "So, what are your plans with it today? Are you going to Burlington?"

"I don't mean to be weird Morgan, but I think it's best for you if we don't tell you what we're using your boat for," Jasper replied. "Don't worry, we're not doing anything illegal, but there are some shady individuals who may be interested in what we're doing, and we don't want you to be compromised in any way. I hope you understand."

"No problem. I trust you. But just for my own curiosity, I hope you can tell me what's going on later."

"Of course, I will," Jasper replied. "Thank you so much."

"You're welcome," Morgan replied. "Let me show you the boat and how it works."

Morgan's boat was a large top-of-the-line airboat with two large propellers in the back. It had a large hold in the middle of the boat, four seats on the deck, and two seats for the driver and co-pilot above the deck behind a large enclosed cage with a windshield. Morgan was also kind of anal retentive, so he spent almost an hour describing the boat, including its gasoline usage, top speed, safety features, and detailed instructions on each console instrument.

Finally convinced he had given them enough information, Morgan handed Jasper the keys and wished them good luck. Jasper and Ingrid thanked him again and pushed away from the marina dock. Jasper started the engine and took off into the open water. Port Henry was south of the marina, so Jasper turned the boat right after clearing Point au Roche and headed south on the lake.

The Canadian tourist season on Lake Champlain was over, so there was not much boat traffic on the lake. The waves were relatively calm, but on the drive to the marina the satellite radio weather station had warned of increasing wind and waves on the lake later in the day. Lake Champlain used to be an amazing lake for fish, with healthy populations of bass, salmon, lake trout, and sturgeons. It even used to be a stop on the Bass Pro Fishing Tour and had its own legendary monster called "Champ."

But invasive species, pollution, and climate change had decimated the fish population. The Bass Pro Fishing Tour stopped coming to the lake and eventually became defunct due to lack of quality fishing lakes in the US. There were no more reported sightings of Champ because the large spiny backed sturgeons, which were usually mistaken for the legendary lake monster, had gone extinct. The lake could now only support catfish and carp as they did not need much oxygen and would eat anything.

The surface of the lake was still beautiful though, Jasper thought as they headed south toward Port Henry. The water was a beautiful azure and the lake was bounded by the Green Mountains of Vermont on one side and the Adirondack Mountains on the other. The lakeshore and islands had stayed relatively undeveloped due to the environmental politicians elected in New York and Vermont.

After about thirty minutes, they reached Port Henry. From the water, Jasper and Ingrid could see a small collection of lake houses, lakeside restaurants, one small marina, and a town beach. To the south was Crown Point, and they could see the Crown Point bridge connecting New York to Vermont.

Jasper stopped the boat and dropped the anchor about a hundred feet from the Port Henry town beach.

"Mary probably took off from near where the town beach is now. That's the center of town and where the old road from Moriah reached the lake," Jasper said, pointing to the shoreline. "I'm assuming she paddled just far enough out to feel like she was close to the middle of the lake, but not any farther than she absolutely had to. I think this is a good place to start our search."

"What can I do?" Ingrid asked as Jasper started to pull out his scuba gear and tanks from the hold.

"Just sit there and look pretty," Jasper said with a smile. "Just kidding, but there's not much you can do. My air should last about an hour per tank. Please be ready to help me out when I come up to change tanks."

"Okay," Ingrid said. "Be careful."

Jasper put the rest of his diving gear on, gave a quick kiss to Ingrid, and jumped in the lake.

It had been a long time since Jasper last went scuba diving, so the cold water on his face and in the seams of his dry suit shocked him at first. But as he got his buoyancy set up and his equipment in comfortable positions, the cold-water shock subsided, and he settled into the search.

Jasper slowly kicked his fins to get a better view of the bottom of the lake. He kept his movements gentle and deliberate to avoid kicking up any sediment from the bottom that would decrease the visibility. Jasper was also slow and deliberate in his movements to save his air. He had only a few extra air tanks on the airboat above, but it would take time to switch them out. When Jasper was done with those, he and Ingrid would have to go to Burlington or Plattsburgh to get them refilled. Jasper was sure it would not be long until the same group they met on the ski jumps would catch up with them, so he didn't want to lose any more time than necessary.

Scuba divers can be annoying when talking about how different diving feels than anything else, especially when they say stuff like "It's like another world down there," but that does not make them wrong. The weightlessness and the silence were otherworldly and was a sensation probably only shared with astronauts on spacewalks. Jasper concentrated on breathing slow and steady. Long and slow inhale…long and slow exhale.

Once Jasper angled his body to get his orientation and buoyancy correct, he started scanning the bottom of the lake by slowly pushing his body left to right with his arms. The artifact could very well look like a rock, but it would not look like the few plain brown rocks at the bottom of Lake Champlain.

The scanning went easily as Jasper mentally gridded off the area under the boat into 200-foot long by 25-foot wide search boxes. He scanned a width of about 25 feet as he moved forward about 200 feet and then turned around and scanned the next grid over. He used the anchor and a few larger rocks at the bottom of the lake as landmarks.

The first hour went by fast. Jasper found nothing of interest other than some extremely large carp slowly swimming by on the bottom of the lake, scrapping up every piece of vegetation they could find. Jasper was a bit apprehensive when one of the six-foot monsters approached, but they showed no interest in him and continued their bottom feeding.

As his tank hit 100 psi, Jasper slowly swam to the surface and climbed back into the airboat. Ingrid put down her book and helped him get the last part of his body and equipment over the side of the airboat.

"Anything?" Ingrid asked.

"Nothing yet," Jasper replied as he threw off his buoyancy compensator and started to take off the air tank. "But the visibility is actually pretty good, so I'm covering a lot of ground."

Jasper finished hooking up the new air tank, threw his buoyancy compensator back on, and jumped back in the water. Jasper quickly picked up where he last ended his scan and got back to work.

About halfway into his second tank, Jasper noticed something on the bottom of the lake that looked different. It looked like a rock but was very light colored compared with the surrounding rocks. Jasper gave two quick kicks of his fins to get directly above the weird looking object. It looked like volcanic glass and its edges were much more rounded than the surrounding jagged boulders. Jasper rotated his body downward, gave two more swift kicks, and reached out his hands to touch it. The first thing Jasper thought when he saw it was that it looked like a large fossilized computer tablet. It had very smooth edges and was about the size and shape of an old computer monitor. The back side of the object was rounded while the front had a flat rectangular side, about three feet wide by two feet tall.

Where did this object come from? Was it really an alien artifact? Was it simply a tablet that had been fossilized in a strange way? Was it from time travelers who accidently left their tablet computer in the past?

These questions bounced around in Jasper's head until he forced his concentration back to the present and another question. How would he get this up to the surface? Jasper knelt on the bottom of the lake next to the object and gave it a small push. Just that small push easily rocked the object, so he tried to pick it up. It was much lighter than he had anticipated. He might be able to get this thing up to the surface himself, he thought.

Jasper detached his dive bag from his buoyancy compensator and placed the object in the bag. After closing the bag, Jasper pressed the button on his buoyancy compensator to put air in it and increase his buoyancy. When Jasper had put as much air as the buoyancy compensator would take, he pushed himself off the bottom and started to swim toward the surface. Jasper was only able to kick as he had to hold the dive bag with the object inside. However, he was making good progress as the surface got closer and closer.

Jasper finally breached the surface of the lake. He looked around and found the boat about two hundred feet away. Swimming on the surface was much harder. Jasper first tried to swim with a side stroke dragging the dive bag along the side of him. It became easier as he switched to putting his head in the water with the dive bag below him and using only his legs to propel him toward the boat.

As Jasper approached the boat, Ingrid got up and came over to the side of the boat.

"Anything?" she asked.

Jasper paused for effect and left the bag below him for a few minutes as he held on to the side of the boat.

"Are you okay?" Ingrid asked.

Not wanting to worry her, Jasper finally tossed the dive bag onto the boat without a word and started climbing into the boat.

Ingrid did not help Jasper into the boat this time. Instead, she took the dive bag and pulled out the object.

“What is it?” she asked.

“I have no idea,” Jasper said. “But it’s not a rock and it’s not natural. Those edges are too smooth, and that shape definitely looks like it was manufactured.”

Jasper stripped off his dive gear and changed into dry clothes as Ingrid continued to evaluate the object.

Suddenly, the silence of the late afternoon was broken by the whine of motor boats nearby.

Chapter 25

"Good luck is another name for tenacity of purpose."

~ Ralph Waldo Emerson

Jasper looked up from the object and saw three boats speeding toward them. They were not coast guard or police as there were no markings on the side of the boats.

"Shit," Jasper cursed. "Put that thing in the hold and strap in!" He climbed into the driver's seat of the boat.

Jasper turned on the ignition and gunned the airboat to full speed just as Ingrid strapped herself in the passenger seat. The wind had picked up from earlier in the day, so the waves were rolling over Lake Champlain at heights up to four feet.

The airboat was not as fast the motorboats chasing them, but the waves hindered the pursuing boats. As the motor and jet boats bounced against the waves, they lost speed when the propellers and intakes hopped out of the water. However, the huge fans on the back of the airboat kept spinning full speed, even when the boat was airborne. The motorboats would close in and then get bounced back as they flew out of the water in the chop.

Although the pursuing boats were having some trouble in the waves, Jasper quickly calculated they would eventually catch them. The boats were faster than they were, so he knew he needed to find a way to lose them one way or another.

"Canada," Jasper said under his breath. Jasper thought if they could get to the Canadian border on the lake, they might have a chance. The Canadian border across from the Northeast Republic was heavily patrolled by the Canadian Border Patrol, so there was a decent chance that they would run into a lake patrol.

Jasper quickly turned the boat toward the north. As he did this, he heard gunshots from the boats behind them. The first few shots missed the boat completely, but the shooters soon gained accuracy as they figured out how to compensate for the rise and fall of the boats through the crest and troughs of the waves.

Jasper ducked and winced as a bullet clanged against the metal cage surrounding the left fan of the airboat. Minutes later another shot hit the cage around the right fan. No damage was done yet, but Jasper did not know how many hits the fans could take, and he did not want to find out. Jasper had to do something before they hit Canada. But what?

The third bullet hit the cage right as Jasper formulated an idea. Jasper turned the airboat northeast and headed toward the shore. As the shore got closer and closer, Ingrid pulled at his arm and yelled, "Jasper, what the hell are you doing? We're going to crash into the shore."

Jasper ignored her and scanned the shore. It must be here, he thought. Finally, Jasper saw what he was looking for and headed toward a small inlet.

Ingrid must have seen it too because she yelled, "No way we're making it through there."

She might be right, Jasper thought, but it was their only chance. As another bullet ricocheted off one of the fans, they entered the inlet.

As they entered the inlet, Jasper slowed down a little bit and looked behind him. All the other boats had stopped except for the one jet boat.

"Shit," Jasper said under his breath. He thought they would lose all the boats, but he forgot the jet boat could still follow them without any issues in shallow water. Right as Jasper turned around, another clang of a bullet on the back of the airboat alerted him that the jet boat had a shooter onboard.

Jasper was running out of options, but he had one last hope. Jasper pushed the accelerator back up to full speed. Up ahead he could see the inlet end abruptly, with the water line abutting against some trees and grass.

Ingrid saw it too and grasped Jasper's arm again. "Jesus Christ, what are you doing?" she yelled.

Jasper looked over to her, smiled, and said, "trust me."

Jasper was overcompensating and trying to sound cool as he had no idea if this would work or not. As they approached the water line, Jasper squeezed the airboat between two trees and ramped the boat over the grass embankment. The inlet bank ramped the airboat high into the air. Finally, after what felt like an eternity in the air, they landed with a slap like a fat man pulling off a belly flop from a high dive. The airboat bounced off the water again and almost flipped to its side, but Jasper was barely able to save it. The airboat finally settled on the third bounce and continued over the grass. It was technically a bog as they had entered the Missisquoi National Wildlife Refuge on the northeast corner of the lake, right on the border of Quebec.

Jasper remembered canoeing through the refuge with his father when he was younger and hoped that there would be some bogs at the end of the inlet. Jasper turned around to catch the jet boat flying in the air between the trees they had just gone through. The jet boat also became airborne but landed more smoothly than their airboat had.

The jet boat only bounced twice and briefly continued forward before it screeched to a halt, sending its occupants face first into the windshield. Confident they would not be able to start the boat again, Jasper slowly accelerated and drove the airboat carefully through the swamp.

“Why did that boat stop?” Ingrid asked, pushing her long brown hair out of her face.

“The intake sucked up too much grass,” Jasper replied. “Those boats can run in very shallow water, but once the water intake sucks up too much grass or weeds, it clogs up and stops the motor.”

“Is that what you were planning all along?” Ingrid asked.

Jasper was right about to answer her when he heard another boat approaching. It was a small airboat with one man sitting in the pilot seat. He held a revolver at them as he approached. He must have been with the original group but split off before the inlet and came around to them from another direction. Jasper had slowed the airboat, so he knew he could not try to outrun him. Jasper felt like an idiot for having dropped his guard.

“Shut off your motor and put your hands in the air!” the man yelled over the din of the two airboats.

Jasper turned off the motor and put his hands in the air. Ingrid got up from her seat and also put her hands in the air.

“Hand over the artifact and nobody needs to get hurt,” the man said as he shut down his motor. The man was tall and thin with short blonde hair. He looked familiar, but Jasper could not quite place him.

“Who are you?” Jasper asked, stalling for time to try to figure something out.

"That doesn't matter," the man replied. "Give me the artifact or I will shoot you both right now."

"Wait a minute," Ingrid said. "You're Joel Robertson. I've seen your Southern Republic speeches and sermons on TV. What do you want with this artifact?"

"It needs to be in the hands of Godfearing Christians, not heathens like you two."

"Heathens?" Jasper said. "I was raised Catholic. You wouldn't have your current crazy ass Prosperity Christianity without the original Catholic Church. Your religion is merely a spinoff."

"That's enough!" said Joel. "Hand over the artifact now!"

"Not until you give us Riley," Jasper replied.

"I don't know who you're talking about," said Joel.

"Bullshit!" Jasper said.

"Do you kiss your dead mother with that mouth?" Joel said.

Jasper was speechless as his mouth gaped open. How did Joel know his mother was dead?

"You know nothing of my mother," Jasper finally blurted out.

"I know plenty about your mother," Joel said as his boat drifted closer to them. "She was a treasonous bitch who would not keep her mouth shut."

"Fuck you!" Jasper yelled. "My mother was a saint and ten times the person you are. How dare you talk about her like that. You didn't know her."

"I knew her well enough to kill her."

Jasper's mouth dropped open. As Joel's sneer opened to an evil smile, Jasper looked closer at his forehead. A scar ran from his left temple to the middle of his head straight across his forehead. Just like his mother described on her deathbed.

As the rage built up inside of him, Jasper's boat bumped into Joel's, making them all grab onto something to keep their balance. Jasper was able to quickly seize hold of the railing on his larger airboat, but Joel stumbled to one knee as his smaller boat was jostled more by the collision.

Jasper jumped on the opportunity and took two large strides from his airboat and leaped onto Joel's boat. As Jasper landed, Joel stood and started to raise his gun to Jasper's head. Using his momentum, Jasper continued another step forward and tackled Joel to the floor of his boat. Jasper caught Joel before he was able to fully extend his arm with the gun, so Joel had his arms pinned to his side as Jasper wrapped his arms around him like a football tackle.

As they hit the floor of the boat, Jasper reached down and grasped Joel's gun. With a quick and hard yank, Jasper pulled the gun from Joel's hands. Jasper quickly climbed up on one knee and swung the gun around to point it at Joel. But before Jasper could swing the gun around fast enough, Joel sat up and caught Jasper square on the jaw with a left hook. Jasper fell backwards on his back, and his head and right arm banged the edge of boat. The force of the blow to Jasper's head and arm bounced the gun out of his hands, where it fell into the lake.

After Jasper fell back, Joel quickly jumped on top of him and started swinging left and right punches to his face as he straddled Jasper's torso. Still stunned by the initial blow to his jaw and the blow to the back of his head, all Jasper could do was try to deflect Joel's blows with his arms. Out of the corner of his eye, Jasper saw Ingrid leap onto Joel's boat. As she landed in the boat, the boat lurched over to the far side where Ingrid had landed and then lurched back toward Joel and Jasper, who were now leaning over the edge of the boat.

As the boat lurched back toward Joel and Jasper, they both tumbled into the water. The water was muddy and warm as Jasper opened his eyes and tried to orient himself. Jasper thought he was in about seven-foot-deep water as his leg fell against a large tree root on the bottom. He looked up to see the pale sunlight trying to penetrate the boggy water. Joel's legs thrashed in front of Jasper's face as he desperately tried to swim to the surface.

At that moment Jasper was blessed by a feeling of calm and clarity. Time seemed to move a bit slower and Jasper formed an idea from the clarity in his mind. Jasper wrapped his two legs around the bottom root he was leaning against and reached out with his arms to grab both of Joel's legs. Jasper pulled Joel down toward him and trapped Joel's legs between the tree root, Jasper's legs, and Jasper's arms in a sort of modified lotus position centered by the tree root.

As Joel continued to struggle Jasper closed his eyes and tried to quiet his mind. Jasper knew the calmer he could get, the longer he could hold his breath. Jasper focused on his mother and his father. Not on their deaths, but on their lives. On the mundane but fun moments they had shared together. Camping trips with his father. Spiritual conversations with his mother. All his family swimming together on a warm summer's day at the lake house.

Jasper concentrated on those memories until he felt the struggling stop in Joel's legs and his body go limp. Jasper opened his eyes, unlocked his grip, and pushed Joel's limp body underneath the tree root. That little bit of effort had stressed his lungs, so he quickly pushed himself off the bottom and reached for the surface.

Jasper sucked a deep breath of air as his head breached the top of the lake. As Jasper gasped for air, he saw Ingrid breach the surface yards away from him.

“Jasper!” she yelled as she swum up beside him. “Are you OK? Where’s Joel?”

“I’m OK,” Jasper said. “Joel is dead.”

“C’mon,” Ingrid said. Jasper followed her back to their boat and they pulled themselves up onto it.

“I followed you into the water, but I couldn’t see anything. What happened down there?”

As Jasper started to tell Ingrid what happened, three bright red airboats adorned with large maple leaves approached from the north and stopped about twenty yards from them.

“This is the Canadian Border Patrol. Get on your knees and place your hands in the air.”

CHAPTER 26

"The purpose of life is not to be happy. It is to be useful, to be honorable, to be compassionate, to have it make some difference that you have lived and lived well."

~ Ralph Waldo Emerson

PHILIPSBURG, QUEBEC – OCTOBER 2035

Jasper woke up with a slight pain in his back. It had been difficult to find a comfortable position on the bench of the small cell they had placed him in last night, but he was so tired that he was still able to get a few hours of sleep.

Canadian Customs had been suspicious but civil when they boarded the airboat. They asked Ingrid and Jasper a bunch of questions about their citizenship, where they lived, and what they were doing out on the border of Quebec on Lake Champlain.

Ingrid and Jasper were mostly honest with Canadian Border Patrol, because neither of them could lie worth a damn. They said they were citizens of the Northeast Republic. They told them they had been looking for an artifact when a bunch of boats converged on them menacingly and started to shoot at them. So, they took off and were chased by the boats into Canadian waters. Jasper then took the lead on the story and told the officers that the empty small airboat had rammed them and knocked Jasper and Ingrid into the water. Jasper said the man on the small airboat pulled a gun on them and told them to stay in the water. He told the officers that the man with the gun asked them where the artifact was, but before they could answer, they heard the Border Patrol boats approaching, so the man with the gun fled into the woods. Jasper pointed to the direction the man fled and gave a description of Joel to the officers.

As Jasper was thinking about it now, he was amazed how easy it was for him to lie to the Border Patrol officers. It must have been the adrenaline or lack of oxygen, but he was not sure how long he could keep it up now.

As for the artifact they had on board, Jasper told the officers that neither he nor Ingrid knew what it was (which was true), but suspected it was an interesting geological stone or fossil that had fallen off a 18th or 19th century ship (which Jasper was pretty sure was not true). Jasper had his Northeast Republic government ID tag, which confirmed he was an archeologist. He told the officers that Ingrid was his friend who was helping him with his search. Jasper also made sure to mention that this expedition on Lake Champlain was personal and was in no way associated with his work for the Northeast Republic or any Native American tribe. Jasper did not want any of this to threaten his employment with either of them.

The Canadian Border Patrol appeared to believe Jasper and said they had captured the boats that were chasing them. When they asked why they thought the other boats were chasing and shooting at them, Jasper blamed general piracy and thievery. Jasper said the find could be worth a decent amount of money and thought that the boats could be local thieves and criminals looking for some easy cash.

The Canadian Border Patrol confiscated the airboat and the artifact and told Jasper and Ingrid they were taking them to their office in Philipsburg, Quebec for holding and additional questions.

At least they were both safe, Jasper thought as he stood up and stretched his back as best as he could. But he did wish Ingrid was with him. Jasper assumed they kept them separate to check their stories against each other when the questioning would begin. They were not very smart to let Ingrid hear Jasper tell them what happened. However, Jasper's story was true until the part about Joel. Jasper knew Ingrid would not say anything different, but Jasper was not sure how long or how often he could keep telling the lie.

Suddenly the cell door swung open. A short but stocky Border Patrol officer walked into the cell. He looked about forty with a balding head and a long bushy beard. "Come with me, please," he said, extremely bored with the task he was given. He did not put handcuffs on Jasper or place him in any type of arm lock. He merely held the cell door open for Jasper, and Jasper walked through the door into the hallway as the agent closed the cell.

"This way," he said, still looking extremely bored as he waddled down the hallway. For a brief second, Jasper considered making a run for it. He was not restrained in any way, and he knew he could run faster than this agent, but Jasper didn't know anything about the layout of the office or how heavily guarded the outside of it was. Plus, Jasper had been treated fairly so far, so there was no need to make things more difficult for himself or Ingrid.

Jasper followed the agent down the hallway until he took his keys out of his pocket and unlocked a door on the right side of the hallway.

"Wait in here," the agent said as he held open a door marked "Interrogation Room 1". As Jasper cleared the doorway, the agent closed the door. Jasper assumed he locked it behind him as he heard a click on the other side of the door. He had never been in an interrogation room before, but it looked like those shown on TV shows and movies. It was a small room made of brick walls on three sides and a large mirror on the other side that Jasper assumed was a two-way mirror. There was a large rectangular desk in the middle of the room, with one chair on one side of the desk and two chairs on the other side. From old formulaic procedural TV shows like *Law and Order*, Jasper assumed the one chair was for him, and the chairs on the other side were for the "good cop" and the "bad cop" interrogating him.

Jasper figured he might as well get into position, so he sat down on the single chair. He was exhausted. He was about to place his head on the desk to get a few minutes of rest when the interrogation room door opened. It was the stocky guard opening the door and letting someone else in.

"Hey, Jasper."

"Riley? Holy shit! What are you doing here?" Jasper got up and gave him a hug.

"Keeping you out of trouble," Riley said, and gave Jasper a playful push away from him.

"It's so great to see you. What the hell happened to you last week when you disappeared from your mother's house?"

"I went right to bed after leaving you. Next thing I knew I woke up tied up in a smelly van with two idiot brothers driving south on the interstate. They must have kidnapped me in my sleep."

"Jesus Christ," Jasper said. "Who were they?"

"They were some goons hired by the Southern Republic. I knew someone was watching me as I told you on the video message I left you on the flash drive. I didn't know it was the Southern Republic until they started questioning me."

"Did they hurt you? How did you get away?" Jasper asked.

"Well, I can bore you with all the details later," Riley replied. "But I'll tell you how I escaped because I'm actually pretty proud of myself about that."

"Alright, go ahead. I guess you earned that," Jasper said, laughing.

"They had me tied up in the back of one of the boats while they were chasing you and Ingrid. Because they were concentrating on catching you, no one was watching me. I was able to slowly cut the rope by rubbing up against a loose piece of metal behind me. Once I got free, I briefly thought of becoming James Bond and beating up all the people on the boat, but instead I threw myself overboard. Nobody noticed, so I was able to swim to shore. Once I got to shore I was freezing my ass off, so I was glad when Canadian Customs picked me up. They even gave me some Tim Horton's coffee. I forgot how good that stuff tastes!"

"So, what now?" Jasper asked.

"We walk out of here," Riley said. "The guys who kidnapped me and were chasing you are wanted in many Republics and by the Canadians. The Canadians know you were on a legal archeological search, so they only want to get your and Ingrid's statements before they let you go."

"And the guys who kidnapped you and chased us?"

"They will likely be extradited to the Republic that wants them the most to get charged and jailed." Riley said. "I already made my statement, and they're taking Ingrid's statement now. They'll be in here shortly. I'll be waiting outside. It's all good."

Riley gave Jasper hug and left the room. A few minutes later, two officers came in and asked Jasper a few questions. Unlike on *Law and Order*, they were both good cops who seemed more bored than anything else. They had a lot to deal with at the republic borders, and this seemed more like boring paperwork for them than anything.

After taking Jasper's statement, they walked him out to the discharge station where another friendly Canadian checked him out.

Before Jasper could ask about the boat and the artifact, the officer said, "We contacted the owner of the boat and he confirmed that he authorized you to use it. We told him we must hold it here until he can come up here and claim it. He said that was no problem and he would come up to get it tomorrow. You have a very nice cousin."

"I know," Jasper replied.

"Your friend took all of your belongings and equipment out of the boat. He said he'll meet you outside. Your partner is already with him. Any questions?"

"No sir, thank you," Jasper replied.

Chapter 27

"Be silly. Be honest. Be kind."

~ Ralph Waldo Emerson

As Jasper stepped outside he saw Riley's SUV outside the Border Patrol station with Riley in the driver's seat and Ingrid the front seat. Jasper opened the back door and climbed in.

"Where to now?" Riley asked.

"Have you looked at the artifact?" Jasper asked, convinced none of the Canadian officers would be listening now.

"Not closely," Riley replied. "I didn't want to give it too much attention while I was with Canadian Customs. They asked me what I thought it was, and I told them you were the expert."

"That's the first time you've ever said that," Jasper said. "Well, why don't we go to the lake house tonight to examine it? There's plenty of room for you guys and there's food and drinks there."

"Sounds good," Riley and Ingrid said simultaneously.

As they drove from Quebec to Chazy Lake, Ingrid and Jasper shared their journey and adventures with Riley. Now that they were alone, Jasper also shared what actually happened in his fight with Joel and how he knew he had been the man who killed his mother.

Riley shared his ordeal as well. The Southern Republic thought he was onto something that had the possibility of shattering their theocracy based on a warped view of Christianity. So, they kidnapped him and tried to get some information out of him. Riley admitted that after they injected him with something, he told them he had left all his information with Jasper in hopes he would continue his search.

"I'm really sorry about that. I really appreciate you moving forward with the search. I think you did a better job than I would have done," Riley said.

"That's okay. I was really torn between moving ahead with the search and concentrating on figuring out what happened to you," Jasper replied. "Did you call your mother?"

"Yes, she says hi and that Dakota is doing fine," Riley said with a wry smile.

Ingrid looked at Riley and then back at Jasper with a look that could have shattered glass. Ingrid knew Jasper had always been attracted to Riley's mother. When Ingrid glared at him, Jasper shrugged his shoulders. Jasper knew they would be talking about that later.

Riley continued his story and said that the Southern Republic had been one step behind them for the entire journey. They arrived at Serenity Village the day Ingrid and Jasper went to Moriah. But then they followed Ingrid when she left that night to come to the lake house. They followed them to the marina and rented their own boats to follow them on the lake to Port Henry. As Jasper was diving for the artifact, they hid in a cove watching them, this time with Riley. When they saw they had found something, they ambushed them.

Jasper told Riley about their encounter with Billy Oscar and his goons at the ski jump in Lake Placid. Riley said Oscar had interrogated him at the beginning of his kidnapping. Riley said whatever they injected him with made him tell the truth, but he was still able to withhold enough information to keep Ingrid and Jasper a step ahead of them. Other than the injections, Riley said they had treated him well.

After crossing the border to the Northeast Republic, Riley dropped Jasper and Ingrid off at Jasper's car, which they had left at Mooney Bay Marina in Plattsburgh. They all arrived at Chazy Lake at about 6:00 p.m. As Ingrid and Riley brought in their stuff and got comfortable, Jasper went into the kitchen and made some homemade Michigans. Michigans were a local "delicacy" of the Plattsburgh area. Honestly, it was merely a spicy chili dog without beans, but they were only called Michigans in about a fifty-mile radius around Plattsburgh. Jasper always kept a frozen bit of the meat sauce in the freezer at the lake house. He thought of it as a family recipe, but it was likely ripped off from one of the Michigan owners of restaurants in the area.

As they sat down to a simple meal of Michigans and beers, Jasper placed the artifact in the center of the table for them to examine.

"So, is this thing alien or not?" Jasper asked Riley.

"I don't know, but I think it may be alien," Riley said. "I would like to get the material analyzed by a mass spectrometer to be sure. What do you think it is?"

"Well, my first thought is that it looks like a fossilized computer monitor or tablet," Jasper replied. "But fossilization takes at least ten thousand years. If it's a tablet or something like that, it would have been left in the past a long time ago. Either by aliens or perhaps time travelers."

"Time travelers? And you called me crazy because I believed it was an alien artifact?" Riley replied. "With our current knowledge of science, time travelling backward is impossible. However, most scientists believe aliens exist and some think it is very possible that aliens visited this planet in the past."

"What do you think it is?" Jasper asked Ingrid.

Ingrid picked up the artifact and slowly moved her hands across it.

"I don't know," Ingrid replied. "It seems manufactured. The front is perfectly flat, like a screen," Ingrid said as she placed her palm on the front of the artifact.

Suddenly the artifact lit up. The flat part lit up like a computer screen. They all leaned over to look and saw that the screen had a long list of flags on it. Jasper recognized some of the flags, but not all of them. The United States flag was obvious, but it had fewer stars on it.

"I guess you were right," Riley said. "It sure looks like a fossilized tablet."

"Maybe," Jasper replied. "But why is there a list of flags and why does the American flag have only thirty-one stars on it?"

"I'm assuming the flags are to help us choose a language," Ingrid said. "As for the American flag, according to our research the artifact was originally found by Emerson just before the Philosophers' Camp excursion. That would have been 1857-1858. If this artifact was meant to be viewed at that time, the American flag would have had fewer stars."

"Meant to be viewed?" Riley said. "So, you think this thing was placed or dropped around Walden Pond on earth for a purpose?"

"Well, there's only one way to find out," Jasper said. "Try touching the American flag and see what happens."

Ingrid touched the American flag on the screen. The screen momentarily went blank and then the room they were in transformed into something else. It was like a mix of the best VR and holographic technology they had ever seen. They still sat in their chairs, but the ceiling was replaced with stars and the walls appeared to be part of a spaceship. As Jasper's eyes adjusted to this new reality, a man magically appeared in front of them. The man was older with a full white beard, a full head of white hair, and a long white robe. He smiled and started to speak.

"Greetings. Please do not be afraid. What I am about to tell you may be difficult to hear but it is the truth. It also may be hard to believe, but that does not mean it is not the truth.

To begin with the truth, the being you see now is not a true representation of who is sending this message. I am not a god and it is not gods that are sending you this message. We believed this image would make you the most comfortable. This message has been prerecorded and sent to you with great difficulty. If our calculations are correct, this message box arrived on your world in the Christian Calendar year of 1858. Although we could estimate the timing with some accuracy, our location estimates were less accurate. That is why we added flags to start the message, so this message could be delivered in the correct language.

From your perspective, you would consider us an advanced civilization. We can fly through the galaxy at amazing speeds and have made advancements in science that would seem like magic to you. We are part of a larger alliance of hundreds of civilizations from across the known galaxy. This alliance tries to maintain peace and order in the galaxy.

One of the alliance's goals is to prohibit interference from advanced civilizations on planets that have not advanced to a certain level of intelligence and progress. You currently reside on one of those planets. It may help to think of yourselves as living in a type of protected park. No one is allowed to visit your park or have any communication or contact with you. We are only allowed to view your civilization from afar using our advanced observational abilities.

However, not all of us believe in the alliance's law of noninterference. We have watched in horror as many civilizations like yours have destroyed themselves over minor disputes and differences. Our group believes these civilizations could have been saved with help and assistance from other more advanced civilizations. Unfortunately, the alliance has an extremely powerful defense system surrounding the solar systems of these planets that is almost impossible to penetrate.

If you are receiving this message, our attempt at reaching you has succeeded. Our only attempts at communication have been through these message boxes hidden in what appear to the alliance's defense system to be meteorites. So far, this seems to be the only way to penetrate the alliance's defense system. However, even these attempts can fail as the meteorite can go off-course and miss our intended planet. Or it can hit the planet, but land in a remote area never to be found.

Now to the important part of this message. Based on our observations of your civilization and other civilizations, you are about to enter a pivotal time in your development. Your scientific advancement will soon make a large step forward. You will have knowledge and abilities beyond your current imaginations. You have the knowledge of the entire world at your fingertips. You will be able to travel to the ends of the world in hours instead of months. Most importantly, you will be able to build weapons that will have the power to destroy all civilization on the planet.

These advancements are neither good nor evil. If they are put in the hands of evil beings, they will be used for evil purposes. If they are put in the hands of good beings, they will be used for good purposes.

All life is good. All the beings on your planet have a connection to the rest of the universe. Each second you are alive is a gift you have been given. No living being is more special than any other being. The enslavement of other human beings, as is happening in some parts of your world at this moment, must be stopped at all costs. You must begin to see yourselves as part of one human race that is responsible for the future of your entire planet and you must do it quickly. All minor differences you see in each other's religious beliefs, origins, or genders must be resolved.

If these differences are not resolved before your scientific advancement gets to a certain juncture, your civilization will be destroyed. If your future continues similarly to what we have observed on other worlds, you will likely organize yourselves in smaller and smaller groups and blame all your difficulties on others. As your planet resources become exhausted and your advancements affect the viability of your planet to sustain life, minor disagreements will evolve into full out wars as each group desperately tries to control the remaining dwindling resources of your planet.

We have seen too many civilizations like yours destroy themselves for us to continue to do nothing. Your art, writing, and music show the potential of your civilization and what it can accomplish if you can overcome your petty differences. We will continue to attempt to send these messages to your civilization, but we are not sure of the success of our future endeavors. All we can promise is that we will keep trying.

We know you probably will have many questions and many doubts after listening to this message. With all our advanced knowledge and communication with other civilizations, we do not have any more spiritual answers than you have. On all our travels throughout the galaxy and contact with hundreds of different civilizations, we have not encountered an all-knowing and all-powerful God that controls our fate. Life can be extended, but death is inevitable for all species.

The one truth we can share with you is that we are all stronger together than we are apart. There is a spiritual energy that connects all of you with everything else in the universe. When that energy is directed toward tolerance, knowledge, and kindness anything is possible. When that energy is directed toward intolerance, ignorance, and selfishness; all that leads to is destruction."

Chapter 28

"Don't be too timid and squeamish about your actions. All life is an experiment. The more experiments you make the better."

~ Ralph Waldo Emerson

Chazy Lake, NY – October 2035

"Fuckin eh," Riley said after several seconds of silence.

At the end of the message, the room returned to normal and the object became dormant once more.

"Fuckin eh, indeed," Jasper said. "Do you think Emerson or anyone else has seen that message?"

"It's possible," Ingrid replied. "Emerson was always a strident abolitionist but became even more so after his visit to the Philosophers' Camp. In addition, this message does follow the Transcendentalist belief that all people have access to divine inspiration and seek freedom, knowledge, and truth."

"So, are we all in agreement that this artifact and that message are real? Or is it some sort of a hoax?" Jasper asked.

"If it is a hoax, it's the best and most elaborate hoax I've ever seen," Riley replied. "How do you explain references to this artifact in Stillman's journal, Emerson's journal, and the diary from Father Brennan? Someone would have had to plant fake documents in my collection of Stillman records, Ingrid's collection of Emerson records, and your private collection of your Father's genealogy records. Then they would have had to dump the object into Lake Champlain to make sure we found it. Anything is possible, but this being a hoax seems very, very improbable."

"I agree with Riley for once," Ingrid said. "We could have the object tested for its atomic composition. Finding elements that are not found on Earth would prove that it's from outer space. Jasper, what do you think?"

"I agree," Jasper replied. "So, we believe the artifact is not a hoax, but what about the message? Do we believe that its message is from an advanced civilization that's treating us like wildlife in a National Park?"

"There are worse ways to be treated," Riley said. "They could have just destroyed us and taken all our resources. That's what the Europeans pretty much did to the Native Americans. If this message is real, it does solve Fermi's Paradox."

"What is Fermi's Paradox?" Ingrid asked.

Jasper jumped in. "Fermi's Paradox basically asks the question 'Where the hell is everybody?'"

"Huh?" Ingrid said.

Jasper continued, "As many stars as there are in our galaxy, a hundred to four hundred billion, there are roughly an equal number of galaxies in the observable universe—so for every star in the colossal Milky Way, there's a whole galaxy out there. Which means that for every grain of sand on every beach on Earth, there are ten thousand stars out there. Opinions on how many stars are 'sun-like' typically range from 5 percent to 20 percent. Going with a conservative 5 percent, and the lower end for the number of total stars, gives us five hundred quintillion, or five hundred billion billion sun-like stars."

"Okay, what's your point?" Ingrid asked.

"Stay with me," Jasper said. "There is also a debate over what percentage of those sun-like stars might be orbited by an Earth-like planet. Some say it's as high as 50 percent, but let's go with the more conservative 22 percent that came out of a recent study. That suggests that there's a potentially habitable Earth-like planet orbiting at least 1 percent of the total stars in the universe—a total of a hundred billion billion Earth-like planets."

"OK," Ingrid said. "I think I see where you're going with this."

Jasper continued. "After that, we get speculative. Let's say that after billions of years in existence, 1 percent of Earth-like planets develop life. And then on 1 percent of those planets, the life advances to an intelligent level like it did here on Earth. That would mean there are ten quadrillion, or ten million billion intelligent civilizations in the observable universe. In addition, taking just our galaxy, and doing the same math on the lowest estimate for stars in the Milky Way, one hundred billion, we'd estimate that there are one billion Earth-like planets and one hundred thousand intelligent civilizations in our galaxy."

"So!" Jasper said. "Where the hell is everybody? We should have seen or been contacted by one of these civilizations by now."

"But this message gives us a possible answer to this question," Riley said. "It's not hard to believe that super intelligent civilizations exist in a tightly-regulated galaxy, and our Earth is treated like part of a vast and protected national park, with a strict 'look but don't touch' rule for planets like ours. We wouldn't notice them, because if a far smarter species wanted to observe us, it would know how to easily do so without us realizing it."

"Think of it like the 'Prime Directive' in *Star Trek*," Jasper interjected. "According to *Star Trek* canon, the 'Prime Directive' prohibits super intelligent beings from making any open contact with lesser species like us or revealing themselves in any way, until the lesser species has reached a certain level of intelligence."

"And we have not reached that level of intelligence," Ingrid said.

"Correct," Jasper added. "But the group who sent this message does not believe in that directive. They believe that if we know more about what has happened to other civilizations, perhaps we could get past some 'Great Filter,' for example where our technology advances faster than our spirituality and we end up destroying each other."

"Okay, what do we do now?" Riley asked.

"We need to share this with the world," Ingrid said.

"Whoa, wait a minute," Jasper said. "Without any scientific testing first?"

"Let the scientific testing happen," Riley replied. "But let it happen in the light of the public eye. Complete transparency. We let any reputable scientific organization study the object as long they don't destroy it. If we try to get it tested secretly, it will eventually be stolen by some government organization and hidden from the world, but if we go public immediately, it won't be able to be hidden."

"OK, how do we go public?" Jasper asked.

"Leave that to me," Riley said with a smile.

Epilogue

"You cannot do a kindness too soon, for you never know how soon it will be too late."

~ Ralph Waldo Emerson

Saratoga Springs, NY – October 2038

Jasper slowly awoke as the light of the morning leaked through the room darkening curtains. He slowly turned over to find Ingrid still sleeping next to him. Her head was buried in the pillow with her feet and arms splayed out like a dead man floating in a pool.

"How does she sleep like that?" Jasper thought to himself. He would have loved to stay in bed, but his alarm was about to go off and he needed to get up. He turned off the alarm on his phone, so it would not wake Ingrid. Jasper usually ended up waking up before his alarm went off anyway. He had been on a tight schedule over the last few years as the Institute had been as busy as ever.

Three years after they revealed the object to the world, a lot had changed. Not quickly, but for better than they could have hoped. Riley had some friends at CNN that he called on for a favor soon after they decided to make the artifact public. Their findings were featured on a weeknight two-hour long special that detailed the artifact, its message, and their adventure discovering it.

The initial reaction was mixed. A lot of people, including the presidents of several republics, called it a hoax at first and worked tirelessly at discrediting their story. But as they offered complete transparency and study of the object, opinions started to change. After the reveal, they quickly set up a nonprofit institute on Riley's horse farm in Saratoga Springs. Ingrid and Jasper moved into a guest house on the property and several administrative buildings were put up as headquarters.

The initial money was put up by Riley, but money quickly poured in as donations, speaking fees, and live recreations of the message were played to audiences across the globe. Security around the artifact was extremely tight and either Ingrid, Riley, or Jasper were with the artifact at all times.

Many scientific organizations took up their challenge and they were constantly traveling to different laboratories around the world for scientists to study the artifact. NASA was the first agency that contacted them. After studying the artifact for over three months, NASA scientists confirmed the object came from space based on its atomic composition. Many other scientific agencies also studied the artifact intensively and confirmed NASA's finding that the artifact originated from outer space.

They also allowed all religious groups to investigate the object, but they required them to visit the institute for security reasons. While at the institute, the artifact was kept at the bottom of Riley's converted below-ground Atlas missile silo. When the artifact was in the silo, Riley would sleep in a special bedroom right above the artifact.

Almost all the major global leaders had come to see the object and listen to the message firsthand. The Pope and the Dalai Lama had also visited. After the visit and listening to the message, they both stated publicly that they believed the artifact and message were genuine and did not contradict the teachings of peace, love, and tolerance that their respective religions proselytized. Soon after the Pope's visit, the Catholic Church officially allowed homosexuals into the church and started training female deacons and nuns to become priests.

There was even talk about Riley running for President of the Northeast Republic in 2040. He had already been well known as a business leader and now was also seen as a great spiritual leader. Riley denied any plans to the press but had been discussing the possibility with Ingrid and Jasper, who told him to go for it. They told him he would be perfect for the job and they would help him in whatever way they could.

Jasper and Ingrid liked to believe the artifact had improved the world in some ways, but progress had been slow, and they admitted to each other that it could just be a coincidence. The US republics were still separated, but relations between the republics had markedly improved. Theocratic regimes in the Texas and Southern Republics had recently been replaced by democratically elected secular, but still conservative, parties. There had even been some initial talks and meetings between the republics about possible reunification, but actual action was still years away.

After taking a quick shower and putting on some clothes, Jasper sat down at the kitchen table with his coffee and started reading the news on his tablet. Even a pessimist like him had to admit that the news was better than it was three years ago. International relations were better, crime had gone down, and environmental conservation efforts had increased.

As Jasper was thinking about having some toast, Ingrid walked into the kitchen looking especially attractive in a sports bra and pajama bottoms.

“Good morning beautiful,” Jasper said.

“Good morning handsome,” she replied as she kissed Jasper on the head. “How is the world doing today?” she asked, pointing at his tablet.

“Better than yesterday,” Jasper put the tablet down. “So, do you think that artifact has made a difference?”

“I don’t know,” Ingrid replied. “But does it really matter?”

“What? Of course, it matters!” Jasper said. “Don’t you care about finding the truth?”

“Yes, with all my heart,” Ingrid said as she started making coffee. “And I know you do, too. But not everyone does. Have you changed how you treat people or what you care about since we found the artifact?”

Jasper thought about that for a second. “No, I guess I haven’t. Have you?”

“No, I haven’t,” Ingrid said. “But some people have. People are kinder, more tolerant, more empathetic, and care more about the planet than they have in a long time. Not only globally, but in their day-to-day lives and their interactions with other people. Does it matter why that’s happened?”

“No, I guess it doesn’t,” Jasper said. “How did you get so wise?”

“I had a great teacher,” Ingrid replied with a wink.

“You mean me?” Jasper said.

“Sorry, no,” Ingrid replied. “I mean Ralph Waldo Emerson.”